CW00523346

KDP ISBN: 9798872629436

Cover design by: Joshua Smith & Olinart

*To those who choose to persist.  May you find joy in the small and simple things.*

# CONTENTS

# PSYCH WARD

# ADVENTURES
## TRUE STORIES

## JOSHUA WORDSMITH

# INTRODUCTION
## I'll Keep It Short, I Promise.

Before you start, let's get a few things straight, dear reader. You might not believe me, but every story really did happen. You don't have to believe them for it to be true. Each person you meet in this book is based on a real person or a combination of real people. To protect people's privacy, all personal identifiers such as names, locations, and tattoos have been changed. I also adjusted the chronology of events and took the liberty of exaggerating some of the banter between staff. However, anything eye-raising that the patients say or do comes directly from my journal. You're getting either direct quotes, my eyewitness accounts, paraphrases, or a combination thereof. The obscenity has been dialed back in order to reach a wider audience. I'm sure you can fill in the blanks.

If you're like most people, you feel uncomfortable whenever you find out that you're around someone with a psychiatric condition. It's easy to slap a 'weird' label on them and power walk away. It saves one from the tedious effort of trying to understand who they are. However, people are more than the challenges they face. Once we get to know each other, it's easy to see that we're really not that different. We all have challenges that we're dealing with, but some are more noticeable than others. Many people with mental health conditions face their challenges better than you could if you were in their shoes. The goals of this book are to show how people are more than just a diagnosis, to break down the stigma around mental health, and to make you laugh so hard that you need to change your pants. You have been warned. Was that short enough for you, dear reader? No? To bad because you already finished it.

# CHAPTER 1: **SCARE** IN THE **DARK**

"NO MAN SHOULD JUDGE UNLESS HE ASKS HIMSELF
IN ABSOLUTE HONESTY WHETHER IN A SIMILAR
SITUATION HE MIGHT NOT HAVE DONE THE SAME."

— VIKTOR EMIL FRANKL

Fighting the urge to run through the darkness, I strode across the Peaceful Pines courtyard toward the Psychiatric Emergency Room. *I can't wait to see what adventures tonight's shift will bring,* I told myself. In my excitement, I almost ran over Helen; the pale, petite, silver-haired hospital supervisor.

"Hey Jay, there you are. I have you down for Unit 3 tonight."

"Unit 3?" I asked in denial.

"Yes, that's right," she replied.

I glanced at the floor, racking my little brain for an excuse not to go. *Come on little brain,* I thought to myself, *find something. Anything. The inpatient units get boring fast. How will I even stay awake?* Oh, how naïve of me. I would soon find out.

Once I thought of a decent reason, I looked back up, only to see her disappear into Unit 3 on the other side of the courtyard.

*How can her short legs move that fast?* I wondered. Accepting my fate, I trudged along to Unit 3. *Please Human Resources, hurry up and hire some more techs so I can get back on the emergency unit.* I tried not to look glum as I—*Bzzzt*—badged opened the first set of doors. Another *"Bzzzt,"* and I opened the door to Unit 3's nurse station. The familiar strong smell of lavender-scented soap filled my nostrils. *Hopefully, whatever chemicals the custodians use don't kill any brain cells. I don't have many to spare,* I told myself. I still don't. Just ask my wife.

I wondered if the overpowering smell of soap was any better than the stench of unwashed bodies over in the Psychiatric Emergency Room, PER. A familiar voice interrupted my musing.

"Hi Jay, welcome to three. Don't look too excited over there."

"Oh, hey Patty! Good to see you." I half-grinned. Out of all the nurses, Patty had the wittiest remarks. Even better, she didn't give a hoot who heard her. *This might actually be a fun shift.*

"Good to be seen. Have you met my partner here, Dennis?"

"Patty, you know I prefer the word *coworker*," Dennis cut in. Out of all the nurses, he had to be most uptight.

"I know," Patty replied, "but I like to see the squeamish face you make when I say 'we're partners.' I've never seen any of my shift partners get so worked up about it."

Dennis folded his skinny, white arms. "That's how rumors get started. I'm happily married and I don't want the other interpretation of partner to confuse anybody."

"Well then, for the record, Dennis, and Jay is my witness, I feel zero attraction to you. Zip. Nada. None whatsoever, even if I close both my eyes."

"Okay, okay. I'm going to go give out meds now."

"You just told me that you finished handing out meds," Patty shot back.

"I ummm... forgot one." Dennis stood and walked away quickly.

"The med cabinet is the other way," Patty called out after him.

Patty was a sturdy 5 feet 10 inches of pure spunk with shoulder length dirty blonde hair. She towered over Dennis. Her wrists were the size of his biceps. She could hurl him across the room if she really wanted to. His glasses didn't make him any more intimidating. *Hopefully, we don't get any riots when Patty's on break, because I don't want my safety to depend on him,* I told myself. If anything went down then this was not going to be a fun shift. I could be wrong, maybe Dennis knew Ninjitsu, but in this place, appearances usually make or break the peace. To be fair, I'm not much more intimidating than Dennis. I stood just a couple of inches taller than him. My skin tone matches the beige walls and I'm so skinny that you can't even see me if I turn sideways. If it weren't for my green scrubs, I would blend right into the surroundings.

Peering out of the nurse station and into the patient dayroom, I saw patients of every size, shape, and color milling about. Most of them looked as normal as the people you see at the grocery store. They acted normal too, reading, drawing, playing chess, or chatting away. A few stared forlornly out the window yearning to feel the wind on their faces. I hadn't truly appreciated the wind until I saw the patients deprived of it.

Recalling the advice from my mentor, Kenisha, I turned to go secure my water bottle in the tech desk so patients wouldn't use it. Without her guidance, there's no telling how many times I would have dranken backwash or gotten clobbered. Stepping out of the nurse station and into the common room, I stopped short when I saw the hulking mountain of a man sitting behind the tech desk, facing away from me. His shoulders were twice the size of mine.

"*Please be a tech*," I told myself.

The massive man turned around. "Hey, are you Jay? I'm Allen."

I let out a sigh of relief. Allen could handle any Code Green by himself with both hands tied behind his back. Surprisingly, he had a babyface like me. His buzzed blonde hair didn't make him look any younger.

As I sat down in the swivel chair beside him, it jarred to one side and I almost fell off. *So much for a good first impression*, I silently groaned.

Allen reached out and held me steady. "Sorry, forgot to tell you it's missing a wheel."

He began to point out the patients with the biggest personalities. "There's Kathryn, don't call her Kathy or she flips and you won't hear the end of it. That's Steven. For some reason, he's attracted to her, so we gotta keep an eye on him. Over there in the corner is Roger. He doesn't say much, so I'm not sure if really just chill or if he's actually a ticking time bomb. We'll see." He paused, scanning the room. "There's the one we got to keep the closest eye on. Ike."

Allen nodded his head toward a man with the same scrawny build as Dennis. Unlike Dennis, he looked physically healthy. He had a white towel wrapped around his head which stood out against his curly black hair and olive skin tone. Like many patients, he wore blue paper scrubs. Unlike any of them, he wore a green sock tied around each of his wrists and ankles. He was also the only one with a disposable glove on one hand.

Ike walked up to the tech desk as if he had heard his name. "Can you let me in the bathroom?" he asked in a monotone voice.

"Sure," I answered, walking around the desk. "I'm Jay, I'll be one of your techs for the evening. You're Ike, right?"

"Right."

I held the door open for him and he went inside without another word.

When I returned, Allen tossed me a fluorescent construction vest. "Your turn, you lucky dog."

Whoever wore the vest got to log where every patient was and what they were doing every 30 minutes. I still had twenty minutes until the next round. I put on the vest and leaned against a pillar in the middle of the common room, giving my knees a break.

"Hey Allen, who gave him the glove?" I asked.

"Oh, man, get off that pillar," he replied with urgency in his voice.

I rolled my eyes. "Whatever."

"No, really, Damian from day shift told me that this morning Ike came out of the bathroom with a tube sock and began whirling it around like a sling."

"You're scared of a sock?"

"It wasn't just any sock, Jay.  Somehow he put poop in it first. Nobody wanted to be the first to restrain him. He began smacking the pillar right there with it and marking it up."

I jumped. "This pillar I was leaning on?"

"That's the one."

I tried to inconspicuously peer at my back to see if any brown residue had stuck to my scrubs."So, ummm, how did they stop him?"

"He got a little carried away and lost his grip. The sock and the contents went over the nurses' desk and splattered against the wall calendar. Jack and Damian pounced on him, pinning his hands to the ground so he didn't touch anyone."

"Well, at least it didn't hit the fan. What poor soul had to clean the walls and floor?"

"Tammy, the director, actually came in and scrubbed it up herself. By the time she was done, you could eat off it. Not that I would eat off of it."

"Wow, that's some solid leadership right there." I thought Tammy was more of a manager than a leader, but she proved me wrong.

*Time to round.* I reached for my pen to start the log. Not there. I checked another pocket. Nothing. "Hold on, Allen, did you see where my pen went?"

Allen rummaged through the desk drawers. *"Ike,"* he muttered as he looked up. "To answer both your questions, our friend Ike is a kleptomaniac. If it's not bolted down, he'll go after it. All the patients here have a roommate except for him. When he did have one, they almost killed each other. Just go look in his room the next time you do your round. You'll see what I mean."

During my next round,  I noticed Ike intently watching "The Bachelor" on the common room big–screen TV. *Perfect time to check out his room,* I told myself.  Upon stepping inside, I found a pile of debris covering the middle of his bed. Crumbs, wrappers, Expo markers, loose change, and an all-too familiar pen. As I placed it in my pocket, I examined the shelf bolted to the wall between the two beds. I found various magazines, chess pieces, paper clips, disposable gloves, and a wheel that matched the chair I had just about fallen out of.

"How the—" I picked the wheel up too and went back out. I didn't know whether to groan or laugh at his audacity.

A couple of hours later, Allen stood and stepped in front of the TV. "Alright, ladies and gentlemen, it's time for group therapy meeting. Like I told you ten minutes ago, the TV will now go to sleep." Allen pressed the remote and the Bachelor disappeared into a black hole. Ike narrowed his eyes, and I wondered what to do if he filled another sock. Fortunately, he just stood up without a word, walked over to the laundry hampers, and flipped the lids up. I wondered if he had the skill to toss his stolen trinkets into them from his room. That would be more productive than watching The Bachelor. Instead—THUD— he punched the lid and—THUD—then the other lid too.

"Hold up Ike, you're going to break it," I told him. He ignored me and continued to jab at the lids. THUD—THUD— THUD. There was no telling what he would hit next. I rushed over and bear-hugged him, trapping his arms so he wouldn't punch the hampers or me. Frustration flickered across his face as he floundered. Allen pushed the cart of hampers into the hall and locked the door. When he returned, I eased my hold.

"What were you doing that for Ike? You can punch your pillow instead," Allen reprimanded.

"I want some water," came Ike's reply.

"Okay, let's get some water and cool off," I told him as I pulled a styrofoam cup out of the desk drawer. I turned toward the water dispenser just in time to see him latch both hands onto the five-gallon jug on top. He braced himself, preparing to heave it onto the floor. I tossed the cup on the ground, bounding over as the jug teetered. Catching it just in time, I pushed it back in place and pulled him away. He kept reaching past me, swatting at the jug.

"Allen!" I shouted. *Where's Allen when I need him?*

"Code Green unit 3," Dennis' voice echoed over the intercom.

In a flash, Allen appeared, bear-hugging Ike from behind. "That's enough!" Allen shouted. Their contrasting sizes made Allen look like an actual grizzly bear hugging him.

Ike wriggled like a fish out of water and then stopped.

Allen loosened his grip. "Geez, Ike, what'd that water dispenser ever do to you?"

Ike turned away from the dispenser. "I'm tired. I'm goin' to bed."

"Great idea," Allen replied as he slowly let go. I turned around to catch up on rounding. I was already fifteen minutes behind. Ike took a step toward his room, then spun around and lunged at the water dispenser with both arms extended, like a cheetah pouncing at a gazelle. Allen caught him mid-leap by the waist just as I grabbed Ike's shoulder, but his arms sailed right past us, knocking the entire water dispenser off balance. I leaped back and spun around, reaching out to save it, but the 5-gallon jug and dispenser toppled over, crashing down with a splash as water splattered down my middle and flooded the floor. Allen pinned Ike to the desk while I set the jug upright. Angel, a tall tech with an epic black beard came in.

"A little late. You couldn't come sooner?" Allen chided.

"Did they call a code because you pissed yourself, Jay?" This was Angel being Angel.

"No, our friend here knocked over the water jug. Just ask Allen."

"I don't know what you're talking about, Jay, looks like piss to me," Allen retorted with a chuckle. They escorted Ike to his room, followed by Patty holding two syringes. I left to grab some dry scrubs from my car.

At 10 PM, lights out, the patients disappeared to their rooms. The common room looked lifeless and abandoned. The worst part about 10 PM on the inpatient units is that the only light left comes from the nurses' computers and the moonlight spilling in from the windows. After lights out, whoever wore the vest had to go inside every one of those dark bedrooms every hour to make sure that each patient was still breathing. To prove we actually did the rounds, whoever had the vest carried a hot dog-sized metal tube to tag the metal disk bolted to the wall in the middle of each room.

Allen left me at the desk to go round on the patients. Heading bobbing, I fought to keep my eyelids open. As the shift inched on, I pinched myself to stay awake. When that didn't work, I began pacing like a caged lion.

"Why don't you make some use out of all that energy?" Allen asked as he handed me the tube. "It's 1:30, time for my meal break."

"Please come back," I replied.

"No promises." He squeezed through the nurse station door, leaving me alone in the dark, wearing a fluorescent vest with nothing but my wits and a tiny metal pipe to defend myself.

I remembered the story of Jack, a tech on unit 4, getting punched in the back of the head while sitting at the tech desk during night shift. I wished that the patients would have to wear fluorescent vests too. After slowly pushing the door to the first room open, I padded softly inside. Danny and Ledell greeted me with snores from beneath the blankets covering their beds. The moonlight glinted off the metal disk on the wall between the beds. I gingerly tagged it with a soft click, and retraced my steps, pulling the door back closed. I continued to plod from room to room without waking a soul. After peeking into room 7, I silently stepped inside. The snoring silhouettes of Danny and Jesse lay peacefully in their beds. Chest rise and chest rise. Both breathing. I stepped toward the disk, extending the wand when a deep growl came from something in the room. I froze, almost dropping the wand in surprise. Goosebumps formed across my arms as my hair stood on end. I glanced right. Nothing. I glanced left. Nothing. A second growl came from right below me. I slowly looked down, raising the pipe to smash whatever it was. After the third growl, I realized it was my stomach the whole time.

*Ten minutes and Allen should be back and I'll take my meal break,* I reassured my stomach. I began backing out when it growled even louder. I froze as Jesse rolled over. Both patients continued to snore. *Why does my stomach sound like a pterodactyl?* I lamented. I actually have no clue what pterodactyls sounds like, but you get the picture.

I looked up at the wall clock in their room. 1:54 AM. *Come on stomach, another six minutes and Allen should be back and we'll go eat,* I thought.

It gurgled in protest.

*Okay, okay, let's just finish the last two rooms and then I can dig some stale graham crackers out of the tech desk.* I paused for another gurgle. Silence. *Now, keep it that way. Last room.*

I cracked open the door to 9, Marco's room. Since Ike had to be separated, Marco got the room to himself, to the envy of all the other patients. After nudging open his door, I peered into the darkness. A bush at his window blocked the moonlight from entering this room. Even if I squinted, I could hardly make out a silhouette in the bed. I stood motionless, staring at where his torso should be, waiting to see the rise and fall of a breath. Nothing moved. Stepping forward, I leaned in. Still chest no rise.

*Does he even have a pulse?* I wondered, reaching out to find his wrist in the pile of blankets. Suddenly a roar came from behind me and a giant blur shot into my face.

"RRRRAAAAAHHH!"

I jumped so high, I almost hit my head on the ceiling. As soon as I landed, I dove for the light switch with one hand while brandishing the tube with the other.

When the lights snapped on, all I could see was the pile of blankets on the bed and Marco behind the door, trying to catch his breath from all his laughing.

"Marco!" I wanted to turn the lights back off so that he wouldn't see me blush.

He slapped his knee and grinned at me.

"You shoulda seen your face," he cackled again and caught his breath. "Whew, I got you good, Jay."

"You sure did. I thought that pile was you dead in that bed." I couldn't help but laugh at myself. After that adrenaline rush, I had no problem staying awake for the rest of the shift. That man deserves a prize.

* * *

You may be wondering what landed me in a Psychiatric Hospital of all places. Think of it this way. What is on your bucket list, dear reader? If you are like most rational people, then you're picturing exotic excursions to hidden beaches at sunset. Unlike most rational people, my bucket list included working at a psychiatric hospital. Included is in past tense not because somebody knocked some sense into me, but because I did it.

At my previous job, I dreaded going to work. Imagine trying to fit yourself into a newborn onesie. That's what it felt like. Wondering where to find something more fulfilling or at least less miserable, I scoured website after website. Ready to doze off after scanning through hundreds of job openings, one finally jumped out at me: Psychiatric Technician at Peaceful Pines Behavioral Center.

I just about jumped out of my seat. *"Here's my chance!"* I exclaimed.

Then I saw the requirements: a certification I had never heard of and either a Bachelor's degree in Psychology or a year of experience with psychiatric patients.

The closest I had was a couple of psychology classes and a few encounters with psychiatric patients as an EMT. I had none of the qualifications but I also had nothing to lose.

When I called, I actually got through to a human being. *Good sign*, I told myself.

The human was actually the regional hospital recruiter, Lori. When I awkwardly introduced myself, she didn't hang up. Another good sign, or so I thought.

"Let me tell you about a few openings in the area that you

# CHAPTER 2: **SELF DEFENSE?**

When I arrived for the new hire tour, I tugged on the front door of the hospital, but it wouldn't budge. Either it was locked or I was weak. Or both. I tried pushing instead before hitting the intercom button. A staticky voice buzzed. "What do you want?"

"Um, I'm... um... here for a tour."

"Come on in and bring your ID."

The door clicked and I shoved it open before it locked again. As I bustled in I bumped into a hefty, white security guard in the entryway.

"Sorry sir, just headed for a tour."

He glanced at the receptionist who nodded at him.

"Okay, go ahead, I just thought you might have been a patient."

I approached the receptionist who sat at a desk behind a wall of plexiglass. She looked at me through a pair of stylish horn rimmed glasses. Her bronze complexion remained as expressionless as if she were in a poker championship.

"Good morning Ms..." I glanced at her badge, "...Griffin."

She nodded in response, As she nodded, her hoop earrings bobbed, showing more emotion than she did. "ID and sign the waiver."

She slipped a waiver through a small slit at the bottom of the glass. It reminded me of a ticket booth, except ticket booths don't have locked doors, guards, or waivers.

As I handed her my ID, I noticed a sign pasted to the glass. "Threats of any kind will not be tolerated." *Who in their right mind would threaten a receptionist?* I asked myself. Then I remembered that this wasn't a place people go because they are in their right mind. My mind raced. *If they would threaten a receptionist, what would they do to a visitor? What am I getting myself into? Oh well, only one way to find out,* I told myself. I turned a blind eye to yet another red flag and signed my name. The stoic receptionist passed me a clip-on visitor badge.

"They're through the double doors in the courtyard." She unlocked them—*Bzzzt*—and I tentatively stepped through the doors into the open air.

The hospital looked like a small fort, with large buildings in each corner connected by tall fences. The open courtyard in the middle boasted a pavilion with chairs, a basketball hoop, and a circle of chairs amid a grassy knoll. The wind rustled through the trees, a sound as relaxing as listening to waves on the beach. Aside from the fences, it looked so serene.

The breeze felt soothing, as did the warm sunlight. I took it all in as I went until I bumped into the tour group, nine men and women wearing various interpretations of "business casual." They stared, intently listening to a massive, muscular man in tan scrubs. He looked like he had stepped out of a bodybuilding magazine. Veins like soaker hoses ran up his deep brown arms. His biceps were the size of his shaved head, bulging out of his scrub sleeves. I wondered how often he had to replace his scrub tops.

As soon as he saw me, the man stopped short his speech and looked me in the eye. "You here for the tour?"

"Yessir."

"Alright, I'm Darius, Director of Technicians and your tour guide for today." He cordially shook my hand, encasing my hand in his.

"I'm Jay," I replied, trying to hide my nervousness.

"That's everybody, let's go down to the cafeteria first."

His cordial demeanor and cheerful voice had a calming effect. My anxiety dissipated. I knew that as long as I stuck with Darius, I would be safe from whatever threats the sign up front alluded to.

"Alright, that's everybody, let's go to Unit One." He held

his badge to the unit door—*Bzzzt*—and we filed in behind him, wide-eyed as if it was our first day of kindergarten. In the first unit, the nurses and techs greeted us warmly. I took this to mean that they loved being there. I would soon discover that they were just woefully understaffed and the sound of any new staff was music to their ears. Patients of every color milled about the common area.

"At PER, the doctors determine who needs to get discharged and who gets admitted here on the inpatient units. The patients might stay anywhere from a couple of days to several weeks, depending on their condition," Darius told us.

Half of the patients wore blue paper scrubs. The other half of the patients dressed just like us prospective employees; in fact, they were even better groomed than one of the candidates, who will remain anonymous. The way they acted surprised me the most. They acted just as calm as the beige walls.

Darius badged us out again—*Bzzzt*—and we filed out. I held the door open for the others but after I passed through, another applicant slipped back, grabbed the doorknob, and closed it fast.

"You worked in a Psych Hospital before?" He asked.

I looked down. "Mmm... No. Just an ambulance."

"Gotta make sure the door closes behind ya, so nobody follows you out," he told me with a bright white grin shining from his ebony face. "I'm Tyrone by the way." He shook my hand.

I wondered what would have happened if Tyrone hadn't caught my mistake.

Our group of ten candidates snaked around the one-story compound unit to unit, badge entry door after badge entry door until I had completely lost my bearings.

"*Am I in 3, or was it 2, or maybe 4?*" I asked myself.

At that moment, I realized that Darius had the only functional badge key out of our entire group.

*If I get lost, how will they know I'm not a patient? No staff member would believe me if I asked them to please let me out. I could get stuck here for weeks.* I paused as it sunk in. *How many previous candidates got stuck in this place? I'd better keep up and be nice.*

Most big buildings have two sets of double doors leading outside to prevent the heat or AC from escaping. Every unit here had two sets of double doors that prevented patients from escaping.

Darius paused in front of the emergency unit, PER, and looked each one of us in the eye. "Alright, we're all going to go in the first doors on the female side and wait for them to close *before* opening the second set," he instructed us. "If any patients try to sneak in with us, just stand back and I'll take care of it."

I secretly hoped someone would try to sneak by, just to see how he would "take care of it." Darius opened the first set—*Bzzzt*—and we all crowded into the entranceway between the double doors. As we waited for the front door to close, I noticed a fire alarm on the wall next to me. *"Whose bright idea was it to put the fire alarm in the least convenient location possible?"* I wondered. Then I realized it could be a means of escape. I really had no idea how much adjusting I needed to do before I would stop being a liability. Darius held the second door open for us and we cautiously entered the dimly lit psychiatric emergency services unit. He then moved to the front of our group, standing between us and the patients.

"It's hard to see at first," Darius told us in a hushed tone, "but your eyes will adjust in a minute. They always keep the lights low to encourage people to keep calm and sleep. It doesn't always work."

We clustered against the doors we came through, hoping that nobody would assault us before our eyes finished adjusting to the dark.

The unit looked like a basketball court without baskets. Two rows of reclining chairs stretched along its length, with a gap in the middle separating the female and male sides. The rows had their backs toward the double doors where we stood. The noises surprised me the most. No shrieks or shouts. Nothing more than soothing classical music coming from the TVs on the wall opposite us, right above the nurse station. In each chair lay the silhouette of someone nestled in a blanket, sleeping or staring off into space. No pacing or pantomiming. On either end of the room, on our right and left, sat a desk for the technicians, one for the female side and one for the male side. The techs sat at the desks chatting quietly.

I panicked inside. *"This is where I'll be working? I thought this was supposed to be a fast-paced environment. This is the exact opposite of what I came for. This looks like torture. How am I going to stay awake for more than five minutes"?* For me sitting around is about as bad as it gets. I decided then and there that the job just wasn't for me, but I'd do my best anyway. I would soon find out that we caught them at a rare lull, an eye of a storm, and that I would have no difficulty in staying awake.

To our right, the male side had a set of double doors leading outside, just like the one we came through on the female side. Between them, four doors lined the wall. Each one had a green light above it.

Darius whispered in his deep voice, "These are badge-entry patient bathrooms. The green light glows whenever anyone flips on the lights inside, announcing what might be going on inside" He pointed to the wall opposite the bathrooms. "That's the nurse's station."

In the middle of the wall, a semicircle of plexiglass bulged into the basketball court. Inside, each nurse had a desk facing out, overlooking the rows of patients. It looked like a giant fish tank that all the patients could stare into.

*Bzzt*-Darius buzzed us through a nurse station door. He pointed to one of the mailbox-sized sliding windows in the plexiglass wall in front of every nurse's desk.

"Those let nurses speak to patients without leaving the protection of the wall. You technicians will not get the luxury of a wall separating you from the patients. You'll learn that y'all don't need a wall if you can wield your words."

I would soon learn how right he was. I would also soon learn that at my novice level, I needed more practice for my words to work.

Darius continued, "One time a nurse opened her window to give this scrawny patient his meds. Before she could do anything, he climbed through the window. All hell broke loose." Darius smiled. He was glad to be out of hell

Our overqualified tour guide led us out of the nurse station. Brown plastic chairs lined the wall on each outer side of the station. "So after a patient comes through triage, they sit in those plastic chairs along the wall. They don't get a recliner until they get their person and property checked just in case they brought any weapons."

My bugged-out eyes met the bugged-out eyes of a short, teddy bear of a man in our group. I could tell he wondered the same thing as me, *aren't the chairs weapons?* He raised his hand.

Darius glanced at our wide eyes. "Jorge, let me see if I can answer y'all's question before you ask it. These chairs got a solid, weighted base so that no one gets hit with them."

"On either side of the nurse station, we have the patient phones. They're much easier to throw than the chairs, which is why they're tethered to the wall. That way, no one more than two feet away gets hit with them." Darius walked across the female side of the room to a door with a small window. He peeked through the window and then buzzed us into a room with a computer, surveillance footage of the waiting room, and a vital sign station.

"This is triage. Here, the triage nurse checks their vital signs and tries to get their ID so she can print it on their wristband. Patients come here from the waiting room or the ambulance or the police will bring them in here. If the police bring them, then the police take off the handcuffs in here and wish us good luck. Fortunately, the next door over is the quiet room. That's a euphemism. It's where we put people that need to be restrained and sedated. There's two more of those on the male side. You better hope you don't need more quiet rooms than three, 'cause that's all you got."

He led us to the desk on the female side, reached underneath it, and pulled out a blue, microwave-sized plastic bin that let out a thud when he gently set it down on the desk. "When anyone gets checked in, we put their belongings in a bin like this and zip tie it shut. The zip ties have numbers so you know whose stuff it is and that nobody broke into it. I'm telling you now to put the boxes back away as *soon* as you get them shut. Some techs get lazy and get this big stack of bins out on the floor where anyone can hide 'em, throw 'em, or leave a surprise in 'em."

He put the bin under his arm and turned to the door behind the desk—*Bzzzt*. We followed him single file into a hallway, like ducklings following their mother. Darius turned to the door at his side. "You'll store those blue bins—*Bzzzt*—here."

We crammed into a closet filled wall-to-wall with racks of blue plastic boxes. The boxes ranged in size from a shoe box to a mini fridge. Each was locked shut with numbered zip ties to identify whose property was whose.

Darius smiled as he saw our noses crinkle at the malodorous blend of sweat, mildew, and moldy food. "Just wait 'til you discharge someone and you get to open one."

We rushed back into the hallway and breathed in clean air.

"Now," Darius continued, "before you open a box, you make sure you got a witness there to see and sign that the zip tie numbers match. Otherwise, they get discharged and say 'Hey, I had a Rolex in here' and it looks like you stole something. Of course, any expensive stuff goes to the supervisor's office, and weapons—" He jerked his thumb back, "—go to the safe in the nurse station."

He continued down the hall. "Here you got the break room where we keep the snacks for the patients. Those snacks will be your best friend. They keep everyone quiet. Well, most everyone. But we got meds for those who don't."

Darius took us to his office and signed into his computer as we bunched around him.

"I got some videos from the cameras we have all over. I'm gonna show you this so that you know what you're getting into and what to do. Now, I'm warning y'all, if you tell anyone I showed you this, I'll grab my tweezers and pull your nose hairs out one by one."

I sure hope he doesn't read this.

A fuzzy image of a room with bare walls flashed onto the screen. In the middle sat a plastic bed with sides flush to the floor it was riveted to. A foam mat perched on top like a toupee.

"This is that quiet room I showed you. And this is about to be an example of what *not* to do. The techs are in green scrubs, by the way, and the patient is in light blue paper scrubs. Nurses wear royal blue. This patient that you're gonna see had just punched a nurse in the face so all the staff were charged up. He gets brought here quite a bit so you'll probably meet him."

The door swung open and two techs burst in, each pulling an arm attached to the stocky young man who followed behind them. As they pinned him face up on the bed, staff flooded in behind them. He thrashed around, breaking free only to be pinned again by two more sets of hands. As he thrashed, another tech wrapped her arms around the young man's legs and used her body weight to keep him from kicking anyone. He squirmed around but to no avail, so he did the logical thing and began spitting in their faces. One person let go, and the patient sat up, only to have two more techs roll him over and pin him face down.

Darius paused the video. "Anybody see what's wrong here?"

Stunned silence.

"He's face down." Tyrone piped up.

"That's right, face down is a no-no, even if they're spitting. I had to do a b-i-i-i-g incident report on that one."

"So you want us to just stand there and let them spit in our faces?" Jorge asked.

"Not quite. Just have two people hold a towel over—not on —their face. Now for the example of what *to* do."

This time a bird's eye view of a  hallway popped onto the screen. A skinny, pale tech in a fluorescent construction vest walked down the hall as he marked something in a binder.

"This is Jack. In order to keep people from slipping through the cracks, each unit has an ugly fluorescent vest and there's gotta be someone wearing it on the patient side at all times. Whoever has it keeps track of where all the patients are every half hour in that binder. They're supposed to do that and nothing else, which is the only thing I don't like about this clip."

As Jack reached the middle of the hallway, a head of scraggly hair popped up in the corner behind him. A tan, bearded man emerged, yelling as he trudged down the hall towards Jack, who turned to face him.

"That vest makes us look like construction workers to some, but to others it makes us look like a big target," Darius interjected.

Jack took a few slow steps backward as the man continued to approach and shout unintelligibly. "CODE GREEN" echoed over the intercom. As the scruffy man raised his fist,  another tech, Damion, came onto the scene from behind. Damion spoke something softly and the man turned around and began to approach him, waving his fist. He put his fist down as he neared Damion, who had his palms open in a token of peace. The man suddenly swung a huge haymaker at Damion's head. Damion dodged it and backtracked. As the man raised his fist again, a fluorescent flash zipped across the hall onto his back. It was Jack, who now had the man in a bear hug from behind. Staff in green scrubs poured into the hallway and surrounded the patient. Damion and a wiry woman each took one of the man's arms and escorted him out of view.

Darius turned the computer off. "When you have a Code Green, you start praying you got backup coming, so whenever you hear "Code Green" you better go see if your coworkers need help."

Boxing classes cost me over 100 dollars a month. Now I was getting paid to do the same thing, minus the hitting back. I couldn't wait to get into a Code Green.

I'll spare you the details about the soul-sucking presentations on a swamp of policies, just because I'm not paid by the number of words I write. I'm looking at you, Charles Dickens. After the tour and presentations, we had MAM certification class. MAM stands for Methods of Aggression Management. If you're like me, you thought it was a lactation class when you saw the acronym.

An old shipping container had been converted into the training center. As soon as I entered, I scanned the room. Just a fraction of the people from the tour were here. None of us stood over 5'8". Everyone but Tyrone wore glasses. I sat down next to the fellow who looked like he had been fathered by a teddy bear.

"Hey, I'm Jay, what's your name again?"

"I'm Jorge, nice to meet ya." Jorge extended a fist in greeting.

As short as I am, I was surprised to see that he was shorter than me. As wide as he was, and as scrawny as I was, he probably weighed twice as much as I did. I looked around the room at the other students.

"I'm Trina," chirped a petite, freckled girl with long brown hair.

"And I'm Brenda," beamed a cheerful young woman with short black hair. She looked like she could be Jorge's sister.

Our MAM trainer, Darius, walked to the front of the semicircle of chairs with Tyrone by his side.

"Y'all so quiet, did y'all miss your coffee this morning?" Darius asked as he passed out worksheets. The students exchanged glances, wondering if they were supposed to laugh.

"Tyrone is a certified instructor like myself, so we'll be teaching y'all today. Now, what are you going to do if someone yells at you, threatens, or tries to hurt you or the people around you? Just watch."

He started a '90s quality training video of MAM's creator and fan of silk shirts, Charles Beckenworth. The skinny, pasty, white-haired man explained that in order to de-escalate a situation you have to engage in conversation. First, point out what emotion you notice brewing, and ask if that's what they're feeling and why. Second, assuming that you were right, ask follow-up questions including: "What have you tried?", "How did that go?", and "What do you think you can do now?". The questions are supposed to get the patient thinking, drawing them out of their reptilian fight-flight mode. He used many more words than that, breaking his method down into ten steps, but I'll skip them since your attention span isn't long enough for that, dear reader. Did I offend you? It's okay. Due to your tiny attention span, you'll forget about it anyway.

Darius paused the video and stood up. "Alright, practice time. Y'all will work together to follow the steps to de-escalate me. Y'all have the steps on the paper, feel free to use that, if you know how to read. Now, who wants to practice first?"

Tyrone raised his hand with a big grin.

"Tyrone, you put that hand back down. You're an instructor."

Silence.

"Okay now, since no one else is volunteering, why don't y'all work together to de-escalate yours truly?" He turned around to face the wall and boomed "I CAN'T STAND BEING HERE!" as he stomped his foot and threw a stack of papers onto the floor. The trainees' eyebrows jumped in unison.

Jorge stammered, "You...you look mad."

"Of COURSE I'm mad! Are you crazy? Anyone stuck here would be mad," Darius shouted back.

"No, I'm not crazy," Jorge muttered as he blushed.

Darius squeezed his eyes shut and broke character. "Oh, someone help him please."

Smiling, Trina raised her hand and queried, "What are you mad about?"

"DON'T YOU PEOPLE LISTEN? I'M MAD ABOUT BEING HERE!" Darius kicked the papers he had tossed on the floor. Trina wilted.

Brenda stepped in. "What about being here makes you so mad?"

Darius' voice decrescendoed as he turned to Brenda. "FINALLY, someone who listens. I'm mad because it's my birthday and I CAN'T EVEN HAVE CAKE!"

"Well, what have you tried?"

"Well," Darius folded his massive arms across his chest. "I tried sneaking out to the cafeteria but y'all won't let me. Party poopers."

Everyone chuckled.

Jorge took another stab at it."What are you willing to do about it?"

"I'm willing to kick that door down and make a run for it!"

Dear Charles hadn't prepared us for this. All his scenarios ran seamlessly. Our heads simultaneously dropped to our outlines, scouring the page for a clue that wasn't there.

Darius proffered, "What are YOU going to do about it?"

Trina jumped to her feet, "We'll sing YOU happy birthday!"

"YOU GOT IT TRINA!"

Applause echoed throughout the room as Trina beamed at her redemption. I began singing happy birthday and Jorge joined in.

Darius cringed. "If you sing that bad, then I'm just gonna get mad again."

Brenda squirmed in her seat. "Are you going to pick up those papers you scattered everywhere?"

"Ah, I was waiting to see who has OCD." Darius grinned. Brenda scooped the papers into a neat pile and laid them on his desk.

"Don't worry Brenda, I would have picked it up after class. Y'all should have seen Nancy from unit 4 when I did this, she couldn't even wait for the scenario to end before running over to clean it up."

He turned the unfortunately mandatory training video back on.

Charles continued, "Sometimes you don't have time to chat. The following maneuvers will keep you and the aggressor safe. You must be ready to perform them at any time, anywhere."

A wild-eyed woman in a business suit rushed onto the scene and lunged at him, hands reaching for his throat. He grabbed her wrists and stepped aside like a matador as his neatly pressed silk shirt billowed. Then he used his ten de-escalation steps, convincing her to try a solution to her problem besides manslaughter. He expressed how interested he was in how her solution worked out in more words than I thought would be possible. I grew concerned that if he didn't stop talking, then she would change her mind and silence him permanently.

The film cut to a new scene, with Charles in the middle.

*Whew!* I thought. *She didn't kill him after all.*

Then he began talking again and I began to wish she had changed her mind. A man who desperately needed a class on acting strolled onto the scene and suddenly raised a fist at dear Charles. Charles deftly clasped his hands together and held them up in front of him. The blows bounced harmlessly off his arms.

"Does that really work, Darius?" I asked.

"It does in the video. Now you get to try those on me."

Not one of us new trainees stood over six feet tall. Darius hit six feet out of the park. Bursting with muscle, he looked like he weighed twice as much as I did, but in a good way. As we practiced the self-defense moves, he pretended to resist. I couldn't help but wonder how far he could fling us if he really tried. Trina went last. Rushing at Darius from behind, she pushed his elbows in order to grab his hands. He held both up like it was a stick-up.

"What are these, hands? C'mon Trina, you have to mean it. I know you're a nice person and don't want to hurt me. Remember, you're not going to hurt anyone with this unless you're the Hulk."

She gave it another shot.

"Look at you! That's perfect."

Trina released the hold and beamed.

Darius continued, "Sometimes people need shots and they won't go, so you got to escort them. When that happens, one of you goes to their left, the other to their right, each placing one hand on their wrist and the other on their elbow. They're going to squirm, so hold on tight. If they dig in their heels, just use your hips to scoot them along."

When our turn came, Jorge and I went to either side and each trapped one of Darius's arms.

"I don't want a shot! No way!" Darius shouted. We pushed, but he didn't budge."C'mon guys, use those hips," he coached us.

We closed the distance, and now we looked like triplets conjoined at the hip. I'd never been this up close and personal with a boss before. Jorge and I pushed, jerkily moving forward like a rusty machine. I couldn't help but think that Darius could just wave his massive arms and he would send us sailing across the room.

"Alright, you look confident enough. It will get better with experience. Now you get to learn how to use the restraints on me." We followed him into a room with what looked like a rigid, blue plastic mattress with bars along the edges for tying restraints. It looked like the one in the video of what not to do. He unzipped a gym bag with what looked like two weight-lifting belts that each had two watchband-sized straps in the middle.

"Anybody see what's wrong with these?"

I had no clue, I had never seen one before.

Tyrone smiled and raised a hand. "They're missing the padding."

"That's right, Tyrone. You get another brownie point." Darius reached into the bag and pulled out what looked like a wooly sweatband. "This always goes onto each restraint first, before they come in and your adrenaline makes you stupid."

He tossed us the other three pads and began slipping it over a wrist restraint as he continued. "You don't know how long they'll be in the restraints, or how much they'll thrash around. Even though the restraints are soft plastic, they can really scrape up their skin." He laid each weightlifting belt across the bed, one at wrist level and the other at ankle level. We buckled the ends to the base of the bed. The two sets of small straps in the middle curled up like crab claws, ready to clamp down.

Darius continued. "When it comes time, you'll take the restraints, lay the patient on the bed and buckle them like this. Two for arms, two for legs. If you like your face, make sure to have the restraints in place before the patient gets in the room. Now you practice setting it up. Good. Alright, Trina and Brenda, you buckle the restraints to the bed while Jorge and Jay, you hold me down."

Jorge raised a hand. "Do you trust us that much?"

"Are you telling me you want everyone to tie *you* down instead?"

"Nah."

"Thought so. Last year I trained a group and after they had me in the restraints, they turned off all the lights and walked out. I was hollering for ten minutes before they finally came back."

We exchanged glances, wondering if the job openings we filled were left by that group. As the boss, Darius would always have the last laugh.

"The thing is, I want you to learn this so when the time comes you can do it safely," Darius continued. "Too tight and you can hurt them, too loose and they can hurt you." He laid down on the plastic bed as naturally as if it were a tanning bed. "C'mon now, it's almost lunchtime and we're all getting hungry."

Jorge and I tentatively held Darius's arms down to the bed.

"HEY! LEMME GO!" Darius jolted upright and shook our arms off. We stood there wide-eyed, wondering for far he would take this act.

"Jorge. Jay. I'm all for avoiding harm, but you can still be firm. You're gonna get decked if you don't hold them down nice an' firm. Remember, practice makes permanent." He laid back down.

We pinned his arms and this time I put my body weight into it. Darius thrashed about but we kept his arms on top of the

27

restraints.

"Much better." Darius was being nice. We both knew he could fling me across the room like a catapult. Trina and Brenda pulled the soft plastic wrist restraints taut and buckled them. Then they pinned his legs while Jorge and I fumbled with the ankle buckles. It was just like putting on a belt. We finished and cautiously took a step back. Darius thrashed around like a fish out of water. The restraints rattled but held him fast.

Brenda turned to the rest of us. "Alright, let's go get lunch."

Darius was not amused. "I shouldn't have told y'all that until after class."

He thought that joke was funny the first time he gave this training, eight years ago, but not anymore.

After we all took a turn and put the restraints away, he gathered us around him. "I really care about each of you. If you have any questions, anything at all, my office is by unit 3. The door is always open. There are no stupid questions, but stupid things happen if you don't ask questions."

Tyrone plucked at the long-sleeved compression shirt he wore under his scrubs. "And before your shift, y'all gotta get you one of these, so you don't get scratched."

Charles didn't mention that. He deceived us with his short-sleeve silk shirt. Shame on you, Charles.

To better understand how it's supposed to work, let's take a minute to imagine what it would be like for you to become a Peaceful Pines patient. First, you got here because either the police brought you or you chose to come. Either way, you would have to wait in the PER waiting room. After waiting patiently for little to no time in the waiting room, you would be taken into the triage room. You would not be agitated and therefore not need a shot to pacify you. In triage, your information would be entered into the computer system because the computer system was working. Not only would you recall your personal information, you would be honest and straightforward with it. If the police brought you in, you would keep calm as they would removed the handcuffs and a tech accompanied you out of triage and inside the unit.

Once inside PER, you would go straight to the tech desk on either the male or female side. You'd get your vital signs checked, have the correct ID band put on, and your picture taken. There wouldn't be a line of disgruntled patients ahead of you waiting to be checked in. You certainly wouldn't be so intoxicated that the tech checking you in had to prop you up to keep you from falling out of your chair. Next, the tech would ask you to place all your personal property in a blue bin and you would do it without complaining or grabbing anything before it was zip-tied shut. Since the staff was not busy breaking up fights, they would take your property straight to storage.

A nurse and a tech of the same gender as you would then escort you to a bathroom. You would be sober enough to walk there on your own two feet. Upon entering the bathroom, no one would slip on mysterious puddles because it was squeaky clean. The nurse and tech would check your skin for any lesions and ensure that you weren't packing anything that could hurt anyone, like a razor blade. After they finished the skin check, you would urinate in a cup with your perfect aim and give it to the techs who would verify that you were drug-free and not pregnant. You would then get assigned a seat and receive a warm meal. You would eat cheerfully, sitting back comfortably in your recliner while waiting for a doctor to take you to a room for evaluation. You might even take a quick warm shower because one of the bathrooms was available. You might even use one of the phones attached to the wall to speak in a quiet tone to a loved one, not someone that you wanted to threaten at the top of your lungs. You would take a nap or watch a movie. You wouldn't go up to the nurse station window every few minutes to tap on the glass until they opened up so you could ask them the same question again and again.

While inside, you wouldn't even dream of swinging your fists, or spitting, or threatening a soul. If you did happen to cause a stir, then a Code Green would be called over the intercom to summon staff. Some smooth talking would calm you down before the reinforcements came. If smooth talking didn't work, then the number of staff that came would intimidate you enough to do so. They wouldn't have to tackle you. You would not need to be dragged, kicking and screaming to one of the quiet rooms. If that were to happen, one of the quiet rooms would be available because they would not all contain individuals even more belligerent than yourself.

You would also refrain from fighting other patients, eating from the trash can, trying to sneak out, pulling the fire alarm, drinking hand sanitizer, removing your clothing, or hitting on staff.

Most of those things that would not happen during your stay actually occurred on a regular basis. That's why the staff from all the units referred to PER as the "jungle."

# CHAPTER 3: **WELCOME TO**
# THE **JUNGLE**

I sat in the hospital cafêteria, nervously waiting for my fellow trainee, Jorge, and trainer, Kavon. Having arrived uncomfortably early for our 6:45 meeting, I sat stewing in apprehension. *Kavon? I never heard of that name before. How do you even pronounce it?* I silently wondered. *Am I going to offend my boss before we get past introductions?*

The sound of the cafeteria door opening snapped me out of the thoughts in my head. I jumped to my feet to find Jorge walking in. He looked slightly less nervous than I did. After exchanging awkward greetings we stood there, staring expectantly at the door. I checked the clock for the twentieth time. 6:46. *Where is Kavon?*

"Are we even waiting in the right place?" I asked.

Jorge glanced at his phone. "Yes, unless there's another cafeteria."

Finally, a short, well-fed fellow sauntered through the door. His tan scrubs identified him as a team leader. They went well with his short, coily black hair and copper complexion.

"Hey I'm Kavon, I'll be training y'all," he stated matter-of-factly. He held out a fist in greeting. I struggled to understand his body language. *Does he resent new people or is he just not a morning person?*

He continued, "Welcome to the team. Come with me and we'll get report." He grabbed a donut and turned nonchalantly down the hall. We scrambled to follow him.

My head swiveled all around as we followed him through several badge-entry doors to the PER unit. As we stepped into the hallway leading to the PER break room, Kavon stopped and turned to us.

"We're a team here, so if you got anything against somebody, you let me know. If one of us is late or somethin', we keep it between us. No need to get management involved."

"Makes sense," I replied. Then I wondered to what extent that "or somethin'" went. Hopefully, I had not just unwittingly joined an underground criminal enterprise.

Kavon swung open the break room door, exhaled, and stepped in, squeezing past a metal shelf of snacks and into the tiniest break room I had ever seen.

A stocky young man with golden brown complexion leaned against the fridge as he texted. A ponytail of curly twists poured over his broad shoulders. On the other side of the room, a tall young woman stood in the corner, her arms folded. Her light blonde hair framed her freckled face. Her expression was just as unreadable as Kavon's. *Is she bored or irritated?* I wondered.

A petite, pale young lady with a pixie haircut sat on the counter, hunched over with her eyes half open. She turned her head toward us slowly as if it hurt. I would soon learn that this was a sign of working three night shifts in a row.

"Finally," she muttered. "Who are they, orientees?"

Kavon glanced at us. "That there's Patricia from night shift. She's not a mornin' person as you can see."

"You come work night shift before you start talkin' like that."

As Patricia stared daggers at him, Kavon turned to the others. "Y'all, this is Jay and Jorge. They're new, so we gotta show them the ropes." He nodded toward the muscular young man leaning on the fridge. "That there is Chris."

Chris straightened up, smiled, and extended his hand. "Nice to meet y'all," he greeted us in a rich bass voice.

"And this is Jordan."

The tall, blonde woman nodded at us and did a half-wave as a half-smile flickered across her face. "Hi."

"Kenisha is gonna come cover you for lunch, Jordan," Kavon told her. He turned back to us.

"Jordan's the only female on our team, so try an' be nice. The rest of us can't do the female skin checks so we're stuck with her. "

Jordan snorted. "Whatever, Kavon. I'm coming back late from lunch just because of that."

Patricia had dozed off. Kavon coughed.

She jolted awake and began to sputter, "Uh, yeah nice to meet you too. Let's get this report over with, and then you can hold hands and sing Kumbaya. I wanna get home."

"I'm not holding anybody's hand," Jordan interjected. "Especially not Kavon's."

"Aaanyway—" Patricia held up a pocketed plastic sheet, the kind collectors use to protect their precious Pokémon cards. Each sleeve had a seat number and row printed on it. A picture labeled with the patient's name and identifying information sat inside each sleeve. As soon as she began pointing to each picture, Jordan, Chris, and Kavon's heads snapped back down to their phones.

Patricia didn't even look up at them as she rattled off her report. "He slept all night, slept all night, won't shut up, you know Billy already, he invited all the nurses to dinner. This one's hoarding food under his seat, this one ate and slept, and this one has to pee all the time. And for the rooms…"

As soon as she uttered the word "rooms," everyone else's heads snapped up with a sudden spurt of interest. They stared at Patricia with such focus that you would think she was a judge announcing their verdict.

"Female Room, April, you know her, she came in screaming, woke everybody up, tried to fight the lady next to her in chair 3A who is twice her size. Male Room 1, Gerard, we put him straight there 'cause last time he punched a nurse in the face and she got stitches. Male Room 2, George, got discharged an hour ago, so lucky you." Patricia hopped off the counter and zipped over to the door. "Have a nice shift," she mumbled before letting it slam behind her.

Kavon took center stage. "Bye, Patricia. Alright, Chris, you take the vest. Jay, go get vital signs on the male side. Jordan, go show Jorge how to work the female side. Lemme know if you got any questions. I'll stock the desks an' then show Jay how to run the male side."

Chris put on the blindingly fluorescent vest and began trudging up and down the unit to account for all the patients. He was not a morning person.

Accompanied by the squeals of squeaking wheels, I dragged a wheeled blood pressure monitor over to the first row of slumbering men. I dreaded waking them up to check their vital signs. I tapped the armrest to arouse whoever lay buried beneath a blanket in chair 6A. No response. I prayed he wouldn't deck me for waking him up.

"Excuse me, sir, just need to check-" I just about jumped as the blanket suddenly flew up and over, releasing a stench of body odor and marijuana. The husky white man hardly opened his eyes as he plopped an arm over onto the armrest. Not a word.

*He's less of a morning person than Chris. Would he punch me for saying good morning?* I asked myself. I attached the blood pressure cuff to his arm. In the dim light, I couldn't make out what his sleeves of tattoos said but a few words had four letters. The machine began to hum as the cuff filled with air. Still no word. *The machine is more awake than he is,* I silently observed.

I watched Kavon sit down with a plunk on the swivel chair behind the male side desk and swivel around to a narrow cabinet mounted to the wall. My imagination ran wild. *Could it be a stun gun? A taser? A straight jacket? Nunchucks?* He pulled the lid down to reveal... ...*a computer?* It took me a minute to remember why a computer would have a shell. As Kavon began checking in new guys, he sat facing the double doors so he could use the computer. That meant he had his back to the quiet rooms and the line of newcomers who sat along the wall by the patient phones. They still hadn't been searched. For all we knew, they could have anything in their pockets. The only thing protecting Kavon's back was a waist-high desk that any adult could easily reach over. Or jump over. *Why is the computer better protected than the techs?* I wondered.

"Are you done yet?" moaned the grizzled man in seat 6A, pulling me out of my own head and back into reality. I wrote down the blood pressure reading and quickly pulled the cuff off.

"Sorry."

A muffled reply came from under the blanket he had just pulled over his head. I pushed the squealing cart over to 7A. Looking down, I noticed a ten-pound plate secured to the bottom of the cart. *What's that doing there? Not to stop the squeaking, that's for sure.* "Hey Kavon," I shouted, "why does this blood pressure machine have a plate at the base? Is it broken or what?"

"No, Jay, that plate is your friend. Maintenance welded it on after this guy on PCP picked it up and started swinging it around."

I sure had a lot of adjusting to do. For me, this place was a whole other planet.

The next morning, the usual flurry of blue scrubs filled the unit as nurses feverishly ran back and forth. It's not easy to get everyone their meds on time when you just found out about them at shift change. It's also hard to find a bunch of new people when you're the first one on the shift who gets stuck with the hideous vest. As I checked off the names of the women sitting in the back row, another streak of blue zipped out of the nurse station. It was a Filipina nurse who looked like a track star except for the cup of pills in one hand and a cup of water in the other. Her jet-black ponytail bounced behind her as she powerwalked by. She stopped in front of a large elderly lady in the corner recliner, the closest spot to the tech desk. Troublemakers always got the seats near the tech desk so we could keep a close eye on them. Or at least *try* to keep a close eye on them. However, the wizened old woman looked harmless with her few teeth, big brown eyes, and short gray curls on her deep brown head.

"Do you want to take your meds, Bertha?" the nurse asked with a hint of a Filipino accent.

"Do you want me to punch you in the nose?" came the response.

"Is that a threat?"

"No, it's a promise."

I smiled at the thought of this slow-moving, toothless senior citizen taking a swing at anyone. Little did I know she would later punch me in the back of the head. The nurse wisely walked back towards the station, pills, and water still in hand. Just about anyone who didn't have the passion to become a nurse would have thrown that cup of pills in Bertha's face and then doused her with water. The nurse's tone and demeanor had remained as calm as if she was just taking an order at Starbucks.

"Morning Kavon, hey Chris, hi new person," Dee chimed. "I'm Dee, what's your name?"

"Jay."

"Well, nice to meet you, Jay. I'd shake your hand but I don't want to spill water all over you."

I blinked and she had already disappeared into the nurse station. Bearing the fluorescent vest, I stood behind the rows of recliners, accounting for patients on the male side.

James, the fellow in 7B, turned over and flashed a brilliantly white grin that stood out in contrast with his mahogany-toned skin. "You musta done something pretty bad if you gotta wear that ugly vest," he announced in a gravelly voice.

"Nah, we all take turns."

"You couldn't pay me to wear *that*. How much do they have to pay you to wear that thing?"

"Not enough. Well, actually I am wearing it so I guess it's enough."

"Well, just remember to take it off before you go out with your girlfriend or she won't be your girlfriend no more."

I had to laugh at that. The tension released from my face. It felt good. I didn't realize how tense I was.

"I'd have to get a girlfriend first."

"Don't worry-" he glanced at my badge, "-Jay, it's not a race. Besides, once you get a girl, you start getting migraines and your money starts to disappear."

The man in 7B was more pleasant to talk with than some of my friends. It was a breath of fresh air. He reminded me of a charismatic uncle I would play dominos with on the porch on a sunny summer afternoon.

The next time I rounded, James waved me over. "Hey, Jay, I don't know if you've heard, but I'm Martin Luther King Jr. I'm leading a group to go march on Washington on Saturday. You should come meet us there."

I smiled, wondering how to answer. "Umm… …thanks." It felt nice to get invited to something. *As exciting as it sounds, I would probably be the only one there,* I thought. *No chance any doctor will discharge him any time soon. Poor guy.*

The fact that James would reach out to others inside this turbulent place spoke to his character. The chaos here overcomes most people, turning them to selfish self-preservation. That includes some of the staff. It took integrity to act on his belief, whether or not it was true. Come to think of it, everybody has some kind of belief that someone else in the world finds crazy. I've seen this daily during the current presidential election. James acted more professionally than either of the candidates in last night's debate. They both lost it, but nobody took them to the psychiatric hospital. Their behavior reminded me of my uncle when he gets stuck in traffic. My uncle has never been to a psychiatric hospital either. That might be because his car has soundproof, tinted windows. The chaos of life overcomes us all at some point, to some degree.

I moved on, noting where each patient was and what they were doing. 3B, Jerry, awake… …4B, Ross asleep… …5B, Fredrick bathroom. As I scribbled, I noticed in my periphery a wide-eyed middle-aged man turn around and stare at me. His threadbare shirt highlighted the gaunt features of his bronze skin.

"Hey! Hey!" he demanded. Before I could ask what he wanted, words spilled all over me. "Hey man, I got five wives. I can give you some good advice but don't ask me how to keep them. I just know how to marry them." His wispy beard fluttered beneath his chin with every word.

"Oh, you must miss them."

"Nah, I get some peace an' quiet in here."

He must have heard me tell James that I didn't have a girlfriend. I wondered if he was trying to rub it in or console me. I moved on, then stood there silently as I compared his comment to my own very single status. I had been in a chipper mood all morning until he reminded me how lonely I felt. He had married several times even with that repulsive beard. Maybe I needed to grow a wispy beard.

Once again, I had forgotten to question what the patients here told me. Comparing yourself is never productive anyway. He probably wanted to impress me; wishing that I would bring him food in exchange for teaching me his ways.

"Hey, slap that window there," came a voice from right behind me.

Turning around quizzically, I found not a patient, but one of the psychiatrists, Dr. Benson. He had a cream complexion and stood beside one of the office doors with a stack of charts under his arm.

Sensing my confusion, he explained, "Dr. Patel is in there. He got me last week."

I froze as my mind raced. *I don't want that to be Patel's first impression of me. Benson's got hands, why doesn't he do it? I don't want to be a pawn in his drama. This seems like a trap, or at least a bad idea. A doctor could get away with it, but a tech? Maybe it's a test?*

He peered into the window. "Oh, he's with a patient. Nevermind."

I let out a deep breath.

Dr. Benson turned back to me, with a mischievous grin. "Next time you round, just go up there and slap it hard and keep walking. He'll never see it coming. We scare each other all the time."

For the short time I had been here, I hadn't seen any staff

member do it.  As fun as Dr. Benson made it sound, there was no way I was going to risk my job by scaring a doctor. At least not on purpose.

*Time to round again.* I struggled to wake myself up after an hour of the atrocious vest. *It's always slowest Monday mornings. The rest of the week will get better,* I tried to console myself. I moseyed down the dimly lit aisle behind the last row of males, marking the binder as I walked. *1B awake, 2B sleeping, 3B sleeping*-it got redundant fast-*4B awake, 5-7B sleeping, sleeping, sleeping*-following suit, my eyes drifted shut.

"HEY! GET OUTTA MY FACE!"

Adrenaline surged through my veins, preparing me to break up a fight. My eyes snapped up only to meet the angry gaze of a tall, wiry man in 11B a few seats down the row from me. The men on either side of him snored. *Is he yelling at me?* I wondered.

"I SAID GET OUTTA MY FACE! NOW!"

"I'm 10 feet away. I'm not in your face," I replied.

Leaping to his feet, he balled his hands into fists and jumped on top of his recliner. His brow furrowed in fury as he loomed above me. Motionless, I stared him in the eye.

"TURN AROUND AND GET!"

*There's no way I'm turning around so he can pounce on me,* I told myself.

"GET  AWAY FROM ME!"

*This is ridiculous.* "I'm not doing anything, I'm not a threat." To prove my point, I took a step back without dropping my gaze.

"Jay."

I turned, keeping 11B in my peripheral vision, to see Kavon on the other side of the aisle.

He waved his hand at me.  "Just come back over here, it's okay." I frowned and backed out of the aisle.

"Hey Clayton," he told 11B, "Sorry about that, he's new, he didn't mean any  trouble."

Clayton lowered his fist.

"We had somebody standing on their chair last week and

39

it flipped over. I'd hate for that to happen to you. Will you please get down from there?"

Clayton nodded and sat back down.

"Thank you. Now I'm gonna grab some snacks for everybody, but I can't leave if it's not quiet."

"Can you bring some chips?" Clayton asked, docile as a lamb.

"Of course I can." Kavon turned to me.

"Jay, go give Chris the vest and cover the female desk." I would later realize my folly. Reasoning with an angry person just dumps gasoline on the fire. My wife hasn't jumped on the table with her fist raised yet, but it was still great preparation for marriage. Hopefully, I don't have to edit that last sentence any time soon.

After lunch, I hauled the vital sign cart around again, taking the men's vital signs. I wrapped a blood pressure cuff around a fit young man's brown arm and waited for the reading to pop up. As soon as I removed the cuff, the patient, Cole, looked me in the eye.

"Hey man, I got a new movie coming out. You got to look it up. It's called 'Horizons.'"

I just nodded. Later, as I passed out snacks, he thanked me when I got to him. It felt nice to receive some appreciation. After I had moved on, he boomed,

"Hey man, what car you want? I wanna buy you a car."

"That's very generous of you."

"Oh, and can I get a soda?"

"Maybe when you're discharged."

As Cole's stay came to a close, Chris accompanied him to the double doors. He looked back over his shoulder.

"Don't forget to check out my movie, Jay."

He didn't claim to be Superman or Deity or a historical figure like the other guys, so I made a mental note to look it up when I got home. Then I remembered where we were. I have yet to look it up.

As I restocked the male side desk, a commotion on the female side drew my attention to the other side of the room.

"I know you're pissed, but let's take a step back, Lexi." Dee's voice was taut with tension.

Dee stood between two patients with an arm extended on each side of her to keep them away from each other. A red-faced young lady with clenched fists towered over her on one side. Dee tried valiantly to calm her. On Dee's left sat... Bertha of all people?

*Thank heavens Dee jumped in to protect her,* I told myself. Bertha sat quietly in the chairs lining the wall next to the patient phone which dangled from its tether. *Bertha must have been so surprised when that girl jumped her that she dropped it. It's amazing how calm she is after that.*

Bertha stared stoically at Lexi who shook a fist at her. Cautiously, I approached them from the female side in case Dee needed reinforcements.

When Lexi finished shouting, Dee turned to Bertha.

"Why did you hit her?"

*Huh?* I tried to wrap my head around how the beet-red girl could be the victim, not the attacker of that slow-moving senior citizen.

Bertha flatly stated matter of factly, "Because my feet hurt."

Dee opened her mouth to tear apart  Bertha's logical fallacy but then realized how fruitless it would be. "Well, why don't you go lay down in your chair so you can prop your feet up? Just let us know if your feet hurt again. You don't have to beat nobody."

"Okay," Bertha replied. By "okay," she meant "I hear you but I'm still going to do whatever I feel like."

A few hours later, all the patients munched on lunch. The hot food evaporated their hanger and the chaos simmered to calm. We had finished cleaning and checking vital signs. Kavon had left with the only patient cleared for discharge. Kenisha was so efficient that the waiting room was empty. She even showed me how to navigate the health records system before she left on break. It took a lot of patience on her part. Now I walked by the front row on the female side , looking for something to do.

As I passed the end of the row, Bertha looked up at me from her recliner. "Can you help put lotion on my feet?"

She lay back with her legs propped up which meant I got a close-up view of her feet. The nails were overgrown and the skin cracked and peeling. She held up a bottle of lotion that Peaceful Pines gave out with other toiletries.

"I can't reach that far," she explained.

My heart moved. "Sure, just let me grab some gloves."

It was a rare lull, the eye of the storm, and she wouldn't get another chance today. I pulled up a chair and began to work the cheap lotion into her sad feet. Her stoic face turned into a relaxed grin, showing off the few teeth she had left. As I rubbed her feet, my stomach growled and I glanced up at the clock. We techs couldn't all go to lunch at the same time or the place would explode into a riot. Jordan had left first so that Kenisha could cover for her. I wished Kenisha would stick with our team, but since everyone wanted to work with her, she covered several units. My stomach growled again. Chris couldn't be missed sitting at the male side desk with the fluorescent vest draped over his shoulder.

"Hey Chris, do you mind if I go to lunch after Jordan?"

He looked up from the computer. "Yeah, that's fine with me." Chris did a double take and his brow furrowed. "What are you doing, Jay?"

"She can't even reach her feet Chris, she's been hurting and it's—"

"You better not say the Q-word and ruin the shift for us."

"It's not like we've got people coming in and out."

"You're too nice."

Kavon came back through the break room door and

stopped as soon as he saw me. "Why you doing that? Now she's gonna expect it every time she comes in."

I froze. I hadn't considered the downstream effects of my good intentions. She had developed a reputation as a frequent flier here. There was no way I could do this if we had people getting transferred, or checked in, or fed, or restrained—all the usual hubbub. Plus, she typically  didn't have the patience to wait without throwing a punch.

"I'm basically done already," I told him, shaking my head at my naïvety.

Chris pointed to a recliner "Jay, I'm assigning you to 8A. You need a psych eval for doing that."

"If you want me to sit there then you'd better call a Code Green." I tossed my gloves in the trash can to the tune of Bertha's snores. *She probably hasn't had a good snooze all week,* I thought to myself. *Will she even remember what I did for her? Oh well, then she wouldn't come to expect a spa treatment as soon as she came back. Besides, I did it so she could feel better, not so she would remember.*

When my turn came for break, I shoved through the double doors and into the sunshine's warm embrace. I had become used to the stench; a blend of unwashed bodies, sweaty shoes, and Pine-sol cleaner. I didn't realize it wasn't normal until I got outside.  A  cool breeze rustled by, and I took a deep breath. *Ahh, so much better than the stale air in there,* I told myself. I'd never really appreciated the smell of fresh air before this job. Glancing back at the beige double doors, a pang of guilt pierced me. Most of the patients in there wouldn't get to enjoy the breeze or the sunshine on their skin for the next 24 hours-at the very least. I meandered over to the cafeteria, walking slowly so I could savor the sunlight.

Inside Violet, a  petite, not-young woman, with a bronze complexion stood behind the counter. She handed a steaming plate of grub to a husky nurse before greeting me with a wave of her serving spoon. "Hi there, baby, you're from PER right? You gonna take this to go?"

"Yes ma'am."

"Okay, you want pork chops or meatloaf today?"

"Can I get some meatloaf, Violet?"

"Sure thing, baby." She plopped the steaming meatloaf into a to-go box.

"And what two sides?"

"Carrots and mashed potatoes, please."

"You got it. How about dessert?"

As I glanced between cake and jello pudding, I wondered how short someone had to be to land a sneeze below the plastic barrier. Jello would camouflage anything that came out of a sneeze. "Cake, please."

"There you go, hun."

"Thanks, Violet."

After stepping back into the sunshine and plopping down at a warm picnic table, I hungrily dug into the meatloaf. I had been ready to eat hours ago.

Cracking open my textbook, I began studying for my Medical Terminology exam. As I munched away, I searched for some vacant space in my little brain where I could dump more information.

"CODE GREEN, WAITING ROOM," echoed over the intercoms. My heart pounded with anticipation. I never heard a code called for the waiting room before. Usually, the patients had the sense to act calm until the police who dropped them off, took their handcuffs, and left. I tried to shovel the rest of the meatloaf in my mouth and spring out of my seat at the same time. As I turned to go, my arm bumped the plate, catapulting the contents down the front of my scrubs. I wasn't about to let that stop me from going to a code. Swooping a hand down my front, I scraped off the concoction of mashed potato and meatloaf juice before sprinting across the courtyard and—*Bzzzt* —shoving open the first set of double doors. I could hardly see anything. As my eyes adjusted to the low light, two techs came into PER through the triage door escorting a tall, tan, well-dressed man in shackles. *Aw, I missed the action,* I lamented.

44

Surprisingly, he hardly even raised his voice as they entered the quiet room.

"Seriously, I can't believe ya'll. Just let me out," he moaned. He didn't seem so dangerous. In fact, he looked like he just got off his 9-5 job at a corporate office. Except most nine-to-five jobs don't have their employees in shackles. Let me rephrase that. Most nine-to-five jobs don't have their employees in *metal* shackles.

I followed the trio into the seclusion room where the newcomer began begging.

"Please let me outta here. I'm not crazy, man, I gotta go. I got a flight to catch on Tuesday. I'm not threatening ya'll."

A few seconds later he took a different approach. "Y'all are going to *hell*. I'm going to *kill* each one of you!" He paused, collecting his composure. "Now will you please let me outta here?"

The staff saw no point in answering. Dee entered the room holding two full syringes while we removed the leg shackles. As soon as he saw the shots, he burst into a frenzy, thrashing about as we held him fast.

"C'mon guys you can't do this, I hate needles! I'm calm- Just let me *go*!" He shouted.

"We can't do that," Dee responded, "Your behavior out there wasn't convincing, Austin."

In response, he sat up kicking, wriggling like a fish out of water. Deandre, wrapped his arms around Austin's squirming legs and hunkered down. Meanwhile, Chris and Kavon pinned Austin onto his side, exposing his hip for the shot. He stretched his neck from one side to another, teeth snapping at their hands like a piranha. Dee took a step forward and jabbed both shots into his buttock. He bellowed.

"All done." She placed a band-aid over the injection site and turned to leave, doing a double take when she saw me at the door. Her eyebrows shot up. "What *is* that on your scrubs?"

I looked down at the brown meatloaf stain. "It's not what it looks like."

"Sure." She shook her head and went back to the nurse station. Austin became very pleasant an hour after the shot. Most people are whenever they're passed out. Just a tip, dear reader, keep us in mind if you need to end a fight with your significant other.

After the reinforcements left, I sat down at the female side desk, pouting over missing the start of the code. As I tried to find a way to position my arms so the brown stain wouldn't be noticeable, a blur of bright yellow flew at me from the right and hit my face. The vest.

"Sorry," Chris shouted over his shoulder, as he swung open the door to the break room hallway. "I had to go before they even called the code."

Carefully folding my arms in front of me to hide the stain, I called out to Kavon,

"Hey, can you take the vest so I can go finish my lunch break?"

"Okay, that's fine," he replied, hardly looking up from the urine drug tests he was analyzing. "Just throw it on my shoulder."

*Time to try and clean off the shameful stain. Bzzt*—I ducked into the hallway and almost crashed into Jackie, the charge nurse whose red curly hair had a life of its own. Though short in stature, she had enough sarcasm for the entire unit. She half smiled when she saw me and I averted my gaze.

"Couldn't make it to the bathroom in time?"

"It's not what it looks like, Jackie."

"Are you telling me that's from a patient?"

I shook my head as I slipped past her and raced for the bathroom door just in time to escape any more of her verbal jabs.

After doing my best, I paused at the door to the unit, taking another look at my scrubs to reassure myself that between all my scrubbing and the shadows of PER, no one would notice it.

I stepped back in and Kavon squinted at me in the dim light. "Here, this will cover it up." He tossed me the repulsive vest. "I don't know what it is and I'm not sure I want to know what it is," he continued.

I fought the urge to facepalm. "Just food."

"Chris said he can spoon-feed you at dinnertime," Kavon replied.

"Say what?" Chris hollered from the other side of the room.

"Nothing," I cut in before Kavon could answer.

# CHAPTER 4: THE **WHISPERER**

*Any more 3's and I'm going to rip this vest to pieces,* I swore to myself. 3's filled the log, each round a clone of the previous mind-numbing round. '3' means "awake, in seat." The numbers let us round faster so we're not in the middle of a round when it's time for another. It also shortens the amount of time one's eyes look down at the page. Staring down just begs for a sucker punch from any one of the 35 patients in here. I gazed down at the long streak of 3's. *Please sucker punch me, someone, anyone. Give me something to do.* No one sucker punched me. *There has to be more to life than this.* An hour later, the only change was a couple of 2's —asleep in chair. Nothing happening. Nothing. *Why did I choose this job? Why?*

Just then, as if it read my mind, the intercom blared. "CODE GREEN! UNIT THREE." My eyes snapped over to Kavon, who sat at the male desk with a line of newly arrived men. A stack of property boxes sat on one side of him and cups of urine on the other, waiting patiently to be documented.

"Chris and Jorge one of y'all go, I'm busy here getting these folks checked in."

I cursed the vest again as I enviously watched Chris and Jorge head out the doors. Kavon's eyes sagged at the edges. He had volunteered to stay late to help night shift yesterday when they were down a tech. It wasn't a good time to haggle over going to the code.

A few minutes later, Jackie, the red-headed charge nurse, burst out of the nurse station and made a beeline for the male side desk. Kavon handed a pen to the new guy sitting across from him.

"Sign here." He began zip-tying the man's property box shut.

"Kavon!"

He jumped, and urine sloshed onto the floor. From the cups, not from Kavon. "Jackie! Look what you made me do, you're lucky I got out the way before it landed on me."

"I'll call housekeeping. They need you at Unit 3. They're in a stalemate with that Code Green."

It had to be bad if Jackie didn't have time for sarcasm. Kavon's frazzled face transformed into a smug grin.

"I'm on it."

Whatever it was he was about to do, I didn't want to miss it. "Can I go too?" I pleaded.

The doors swung open and Chris and Jorge came back inside. "Kavon!" Chris shouted, "The supervisor wants you over there *now*."

"Okay, Jay, since they're back you can come. You need to learn how it's done anyhow."

We shoved the doors open and jogged through the courtyard.

"Now Jay, I want you to stay in the background, stay where you can see me and I'll explain when it's over."

"Sounds good." My curiosity shuddered with excitement like a toddler on Christmas Day. As I ran, I heard a clatter behind me. My jogging had jostled my scissors out of my pocket. I bounded back, scooped them up, and sped up to tag behind Kavon.

Jack opened the outer door to Unit 3 and held it open for us. Sweat beaded across his forehead."Thanks for coming, Kavon."

"No problem, Jack."

"Just be careful, he's got a nasty MRSA infection on his arm." Jack glanced over at me. "You planning on stabbing someone with those scissors?"

I shook my head and avoided eye contact while I sheepishly shoved them back into my pocket. *Bzzt-* Kavon opened the second set of double doors and waved me through. I rushed in, bumping face first into the back of a mountain of a man.

"S-sorry, Allen," I stuttered.

Allen turned and glanced down at me through his glasses. He waved a hand as if swatting a fly and  rolled his eyes before placing a massive hand over my shoulder.

"Jay, you just about made me jump outta my skin."

"Shhhhh!" Chantelle waved a hand at us. Out of the seven of us techs crowded in there, Chantelle was the smallest by far but she had the most swagger to make up for it. She had black braids pulled back in a ponytail and a copper complexion.

*Why are they all bunched in the entryway?* I wondered. Standing on tiptoe, I peered over their shoulders. I still had no idea why but I felt the heat from the palpable tension in the room.

Once bustling with patients, Unit 3  now looked like a ghost town. Every bedroom door lining the common area was shut tight. A tan, husky man paced around a table on the other side of the room. With his sun-bleached hair, he looked like he had just got back from the beach, except that most people don't look ready for a cage match when they come from the beach.  He clenched his fists and glowered at us, posturing at everyone that stood between him and the exit.

"I've had enough of this #%&@!" He roared.

He took a step towards us, and a couple of staff in front back peddled, pressing us even tighter together.

"JUST LET ME OUT!"

This was nothing like the videos Darius showed us. *Aren't we supposed to swarm over the aggressor like wasps?* I wanted to ask. Then I noticed a patchy scab on his forearm. That must be the MRSA infection that had everyone cowered in the corner. My mind raced for a solution. *Maybe we can put on gowns to protect ourselves. No, he'd just rip them. I wonder if we could get two people holding a blanket get on either side of him and wrap him up so we could pin him down without touching his arm…*

"ANSWER ME!" his thunderous voice shook me from my thoughts.

"You LET ME OUT or I'm gonna come at you, I don't care how many a y'all there are!" he growled.

Chantelle, the only one in the front who hadn't back peddled, spoke up, her arms folded in front of her chest.

"We don't mean you any harm, sir. We're only trying to help you. You know that's not an option." her voice had only a hint of exasperation. They had been trying to talk him down for half an hour.

Clyde whipped off his shirt, threw it on the ground, and stomped on it.

"Anybody who comes closer is getting punched in the *face*. I swear it."

"Where's Kavon when you need him?" Chantelle muttered.

"Probably in the cafeteria helping himself to thirds," Deandre piped up. Chantelle turned back at him and glared. "This ain't the time for that, Dre."

"Hey, I heard that."

Chantelle jumped.

"Calm down girl, I'm right here, you just got to let me through," Kavon said.

Deandre snorted. "You could get through if you stopped eatin' so much,"

Kavon stepped forward and looked Deandre in the eye. "I could get through if you weren't back peddling."

Before Deandre could reply, Chantelle grabbed Kavon's wrist, yanked him forward to the front row and shoved. Kavon popped out of the crowd and into no man's land. It reminded me of a scene from the nature channel where a flock of penguins pushes one of their own into the water to see if it's safe from hungry sea lions.

"Go work your magic," she whispered.

Crazy-eyed Clyde looked over at the newcomer.

"I got a can of whoop ass just for *you*."

"Clyde! C'mon, brother. Don't you remember me from back from PER? I thought we was cool." Kavon stepped closer and whispered, "Why have a can of whoop ass when you can have a can of soda?"

Clyde chuckled. "Oh yeah?"

"Yeah. But look, brother, I've been standing all day, why don't we sit down at the table over there and you can tell me what's up?"

"Okay." Clyde turned to glower again at the wall of staff who had crept closer to him. They bunched back together by the door. "But I don't want them around."

Kavon glanced over at the group.

"Don't y'all have some work to do? Go on, get back to your units."

Chantelle threw her hands up in exasperation "But-"

"Clyde's cooled down, right Clyde?"

"Yeah. Sorry about that, I lost it back there."

"No worries, I know you're hungry, brother."

"Nah, it's because they won't let me get seconds. Look at me. I'm bigger than everyone else but they won't give me more food than anyone else until an hour later. I hate this #%&@ing place." He spat on the floor. "I wouldn't mind if you stick around here though."

"I can stay for a minute now that things are calm." Kavon waved us away. "In fact, you cooled off so much you probably freezing by now."

Clyde took the cue to pick up his shirt off the ground and put it back on. Ray opened the door and humbled, the rest of us began to trickle out. If we had tails, they would have been between our legs. Kavon did in one minute what nine of us combined couldn't do in hours.

"Hold up, not you Jay, go grab some bandages so we can cover his arm back up," Kavon called out. Clyde led Kavon to his room. The rooms were set up for two patients each, but Clyde was an infection risk so he got the entire room to himself.

As I grabbed some bandages, I prayed Kavon would be conscious when I got back to him. Ever so slowly, I tentatively poked my head through Clyde's bedroom door. Clyde sat on the bed, munching on Lays as docile as a lamb. It was like watching Mr. Hyde turn back into Dr. Jekyll.  Patients weren't allowed to bring food into their rooms, but I wasn't about to kick the hornet's nest. Kavon took the bandages, patched Clyde's arm, and then pulled off his latex gloves. He shot them like a rubber band into the trash can.

"I'll be back in a minute, Clyde."

"Thanks, I'm not going anywhere, Kavon." We stepped out of the unit and into the blinding sunlight.

"I'm thirsty. Let's drop by the cafeteria," Kavon told me.

Inside the cafeteria, Kavon filled a couple of cups of Sprite at the soda machine. (I expect a commission for the references.)

"How'd he steal those chips?"

"He didn't." Kavon snapped the lids on.

"Get one for you too."

I began filling up a cup with juice as I tried to fathom what he meant. The sticky wet of the juice overflowing onto my hand brought me back out of my head. Kavon was already at the door. I scrambled to catch up.  When we stepped outside,  I turned right to go back to PER.

Eventually, I realized  Kavon wasn't following me. It took longer than I care to say. Turning around, I saw him headed in the opposite direction.

"Hey, boss, are you going on break?"

"No, where you going?"

"PER, I thought we were gonna go back to help Chris and Jordan?"

"That can wait. I got work to do back at three."

I stood there, even more confused than before.

"And I still want you to come with me."

We stepped back into unit three and walked back into Clyde's room. *Kavon must've dropped something in there,* I silently assumed, *but that's just cruel to hold that ice-cold soda in front of him.*

Kavon handed the cup to Clyde and my eyebrows hopped up.

"Here's your Sprite, mixed with lemonade, just the way you like it."

Clyde grinned. "You remembered? Thanks, Kavon." He took a sip. "Again, I'm sorry about... ...what I said to you."

"No worries, brother. You were just hungry." As we left, I stuttered as a thousand questions fought to come out of my mouth at the same time.

"H-how?"

Kavon chuckled.

"You heard Chantelle, it's magic. They call me the whisperer 'cause I can get them to calm down when no one else can. They'll even call me in before they call a code."

He had my full attention. I stared back, waiting silently for nuggets of wisdom.

"Look, little man, if you force people, they'll always push back. So you got to find out what they want and work with them. They come in and we take so much from them, their property, their privacy, their phone, fresh air, creature comforts, even their shoe laces. Hell, I'd be pissed off too. You give them something back,  make life a little easier for them, and they'll make life a whole lot easier for you too."

"But aren't you just encouraging him to act out every time he wants a soda?"

"He could say the same thing, Jay. If he was calm and quiet he would just be encouraging staff to keep ignoring him. He was mad because he was supposed to go to the cafeteria for lunch but his nurse, Bridgette, found a candy wrapper in his room and wouldn't let him go with the others."

"Just a candy wrapper? You really believe that?"

"Wait 'til you meet Bridgette. Anyway, if we work with each other, then at the end of the day everybody goes home safe. It was so much easier when they let patients smoke here. I don't smoke but I would just carry a carton of cigs in my pocket. One time this guy bigger than Clyde would not put on his clothes and come out of the bathroom. They called a code but nobody would go further than the doorway 'cause they didn't want to get stuck inside with this naked giant. The directors were pulling out their hair. After an hour they called me in. I walked straight into that bathroom, said what's up and slapped two cigs on the counter. We both laughed an' he said okay and he got dressed and came out nice and quiet. Took me thirty seconds. If they called me earlier they woulda saved hours." He paused. "Now just keep in mind, not everybody thinks this way. Some people get mad when they see it. They tell me, 'You shouldn't be bribing patients.' I don't see it as a bribe, Jay, I see it as an investment. Call it what you want, it still works. Besides, the PER director, Katie is cool with it and she's the top dog here. A lot of it's common sense to me but I guess the others are too stuck up to realize it."

"Well, I'd like to learn some magic from you."

"Alright, you got the next troublemaker that comes in. I'll go with you."

After clocking out for the shift, I sat in my car under the light of the moon, hungry and exhausted. All I could think was, *I can't wait to see what happens tomorrow.*

# CHAPTER 5: **DELUGE** OF **DELUSIONS**

The next morning would bore you to tears so let's skip that part and get to the good stuff. I headed back to PER after finishing lunch, this time without spilling anything on my scrubs. *Bzzzt*—I shoved open the double doors. As my eyes adjusted to the dim light, I wondered if I had wandered into the wrong unit. Everyone was snoozing, or at least acted like it. *I can't believe it,* I thought to myself as I sat down behind the male side desk. Then I noticed a shuffling between the rows of the male side. Someone or something was making its way right toward me. I tensed, ready to take on whatever came at me. I squinted through the dark. *What-What is this, some kind of prank?* I wondered in surprise.

A hefty Hispanic woman plodded on hands and knees toward me. Her blue paper scrubs rustled with each step. *What does she plan on doing?* I wondered as I slowly stood and walked around the desk. I didn't want to find out what would happen if she woke a bunch of edgy, cranky men. I had to intervene right away without waking any of them. She was halfway down the row now, with 6 men seated between us. Anything could happen before I got to her. Quietly, I stepped over between the rows of snoozing men.

"Hey, stand up. Please," I whisper-shouted, "the floor is filthy." Her eyes met mine and she scampered along a few more paces. "Come sit over here, we got snacks at the desk." She stood. She was barely taller than the recliners.

Back at the desk, I dug out some granola bars, and she merrily ripped one open with her teeth. "Why were you crawling around over there?" I tried not to sound too surprised.

"I want to be like a dog."

I stared back at her blankly. "A dog?"

"Because dogs aren't scared."

Taken aback, I nodded my head. That made sense, oddly enough. I pictured myself getting up the courage to ask a woman for her number and approaching her on all fours like a dog to boost my confidence. I didn't understand much about women, but I was pretty sure that wouldn't end well.

"You felt more scared over there on the female side?"

She nodded.

"You feel safe right here next to me?"

She nodded again.

I shook my head. It would be a stretch to say I stood 5'8" tall and weighed 145 pounds. The average size of the guys slumbering around us was probably six foot and two hundred pounds. "You sure about that?"

She nodded again. "I don't like people sitting behind me." I kept expecting her to turn in her chair to growl and bark at the people behind her.

"So that means you're done acting like a dog?" Another nod. "And you're not planning on doing anything else that dogs tend to do besides going around on all fours?"

She nodded again. "I'm done for now."

I let out a sigh of relief. I had feared that she planned to mark her territory. "I'm Jay, what's your name?"

"Maria." I glanced at her ID band to verify she was actually a Maria. In the dim light, she looked just like my mom's best friend.

Maria looked over her shoulder and then back at me. "Thank you for the granola bar. How is your day?" I blinked.

"You're the first person to ask me that today. It's-It's going alright."

Jackie strode through the double doors, carrying a Red Bull in one hand as casually as if she was at a family barbeque.

Thud. My hand hit my forehead as I groaned to myself, *Why? Why? Why? She knows better than that.* If any patient in the room saw that drink, they'd plead for one too, and it would catch on like wildfire. We wouldn't hear the end of it for the rest of the shift.

"Hey Jackie, where-"

Maria stood up and stood face to face with Jackie. She looked like a prizefighter posturing to intimidate their opponent. Actually, she was much shorter, so it was more like face to shoulder.

"If you drink that, I'm sending you to hell," Maria told her.

Jackie's brow furrowed as she clumsily slipped the drink behind her back. "Say what?"

"I am God and I'm telling you Red Bull is bad for you. If you drink that then I'm sending you to hell."

My guffaw didn't break Maria's intense stare.

"That's fine with me." Jackie walked right past without looking back

Maria followed her with her fiery gaze.

"I'll save you a seat, Jay," Jackie shouted as she swung open the nurse station door, looked back at us, and took a big gulp before disappearing inside.

I let out a sigh of relief. The one patient that noticed the Red Bull didn't even like to see it. Jackie could have started a riot. I turned back to the Deity.

"Why don't you have a seat, Maria?" She sat down with a plop before glaring back over at the nurse station.

"She's lucky I'm feeling merciful today."

Kavon walked over and dropped a blue property box on the desk with a thud. Maria jumped.

"Oh, sorry 'bout that," he apologized, "Hey Jay, I need you to run this down to 3."

"You got it. Oh, and Kavon, can you put her in a quiet room? I don't want anyone to swing at her." There was no telling what it took for her to send anyone else to hell.

"Yeah, in a minute, as long as we don't need it for somebody else."

*Bzzt*-I badged the double doors open and turned to make

sure no one would follow me into the breezeway.  Maria left her seat and began crawling again between the rows back to the female side.

Kavon's eyes widened. "Scratch that. Less than a minute."

I returned to a relatively peaceful PER. Finally, the break I needed. My feet ached from standing so much.  I sat down behind the male desk and kicked back.

"Get your FOOT off my SEAT!"

I stood up on my aching feet and saw a man with a white wispy beard that contrasted with his copper complexion. Gerald. He'd been quiet until now.  Gerald sat up in his recliner in the middle of the back row, staring down his stocky neighbor, Brad.

"Chill out man, it's not even on your seat," the white young buck replied.

In response, the old man spat in his face.

*Why did this have to start right in the middle of all the sleeping patients?* I complained to myself. I bounded over as Brad stood up and held up a fist in Gerald's face. Brad raised his middle finger.

"Take it easy," Kavon boomed as he sprinted from the other side of the room. Brad turned to see who shouted and in a flash the old man pounced on him, pushing Brad back down into his recliner. Gerald pinned Brad's arm down with one hand and raised the other in a fist.

"Hey! Hold up!" I shouted, working my way between the rows as Mr. Wispy Beard hammer fisted the young buck. I lunged at Gerald and wrapped my arms around his torso. He turned to hammer fist me too, but I pressed my face into his shoulder so he couldn't land a decent punch. Holding him tight, I pivoted, pulling him off the chair onto his feet and away from Brad.  Out of the corner of my eye, I saw Brad leap up, fists raised only to get bear hugged him from behind by Kavon.

"CODE GREEN PER" echoed around us as we fought to keep both men under control. The doors burst open and dozens of footsteps clattered towards us.  Gerald stopped squirming and my grip loosened. As soon as I relaxed my grip, the old man twisted around and clawed at my face with both hands. I ducked and got him in a clinch, regaining control. Undeterred, he flailed with all his might and we stumbled to the ground. Trapping his arms behind him, I put him in a wrestling hold that kept him face up.

*Darius better be proud of that,* I told myself.

As a wall of green scrubs closed in on us, Gerald began spitting madly in every direction. "PTEW! PTEW! PTEW!PTEW!"

Holding him tight, I turned my face away out of the splash zone as the rest of the staff backed away.

Gerald kept going like a fully automatic, "PTEW!PTEW! PTEW!"

He ran out of spittle, but that didn't stop him from trying. By now it was just puffs of air. Chris pinned his shoulders down while Jack pinned his legs. Deandre reached down and helped me up.

"Man, he scratched you up pretty good."

"Yeah, I need to go wash up." I tried not to think about what diseases he might have been harboring under those nails. "What happened to Kavon?"

I turned to see a swarm of green escorting Mr. Spitter to the quiet room. On the other side of the unit stood Kavon, holding back-*Maria of all people?* She glared at the quiet room as the door slammed shut.

"Pinche pendejo!" she swore.

"Easy now Maria, we got a quiet room on the other side just for you," Kavon told her. He turned to me."She just about jumped old school when she saw him scratch you. I had to let go of the other guy and hold her back instead."

Surprised, I wondered if I should say thank you or not.

In the bathroom mirror, I saw a couple red lines of broken skin stretching from my temple down to the corner of my mouth. I shrugged. Deandre made it sound like it was oozing blood. I rubbed soap into my face and rinsed it a couple times before going right back out to the patient floor. Kavon raised an eyebrow.

"Why don't you take a break?"

"I'm fine. Besides, it's time to pass out dinner."

"Well then, you take the vest and catch your breath."

As I rounded, I peered through the window of the quiet room assigned to Maria. A couple of sticks of Peaceful Pines deodorant lay open on the floor. She stared blankly at the wall, her face and arms covered in white streaks. She then uncapped another stick and began smearing it on her neck. *Maybe she wants camouflage to keep safe?* I mused. *Whatever it is, I hope it's not war paint.*

She was sick, but that didn't erase her virtues. She had to be the bravest, most compassionate one in PER that day. *I sure hope she gets better soon,* I told myself. *We need more people like her in the world.*

I slowly walked back to PER through the courtyard, savoring the fresh air. I saw a big man in a maroon polo step out of PER and hold the door open. The people in maroon always did the nonemergency transports to other institutions. Some patients still needed in-patient treatment beyond what Peaceful Pines had to offer.

Kavon came out escorting someone wrapped up in what looked like a giant pillowcase pulled over their body . It had a hole in the top large enough for their head to poke through, leaving both arms pinned to their sides. The legs came out of the large hole in the bottom and a strap ran between them legs, connecting the front to the back so they wouldn't wriggle out.

*I've never seen them discharge anyone in that contraption before. What did that patient do in the last 10 minutes to land themselves there?* I wondered. *Something pretty violent, that's for sure. I sure hope whoever it is doesn't trip 'cause she's got no way to catch herself.*

As I drew nearer, they stopped at the back gate, so Kavon

could buzz it open and I got a look at the patient's face, which looked cool as a cucumber. *Maria?*

"Kavon, where's she going? I mean, what'd she do? She hasn't hurt anybody." I shouted across the courtyard.

"Terrel here," he nodded at the big man in maroon, "is gonna take her to the state hospital. They got a long-term in-patient bed for her there. They won't accept psychotic patients without this get-up." I imagined how I would feel if I were a woman being led around by big men with my arms pinned to my sides. Anyone in their right mind would have a panic attack. *Please get well soon, Maria,* I silently pleaded.

I stood on the inside of the gate as she stepped up into the van and Terrel followed to buckle her seatbelt. I waved goodbye, unsure if she recognized me. Terrel stepped out, slammed the door, and jumped in the driver's seat.

"Good luck," Kavon shouted. "And don't take your eye off the rearview mirror!"

"Whatever, Kavon." Terrel waved at Kavon as he backed up. I couldn't tell how many fingers he was waving with.

As Kavon came back in through the gate—*Bzzzt*—he chuckled. "You hear what happened last week to one of them drivers?"

"No."

"He was driving this big guy in one of them straight jackets. They're halfway to the hospital when the driver looks in the rearview mirror and sees big boy taking the whole thing off and getting out of his seat."

"...and?" I had no idea what I would do if I were the driver. Actually, knowing my poor multitasking skills, I probably would have crashed.

"That driver pulled over, jumped out, and booked it, heh heh."

I froze in place as my mind raced. *What about my friends in that area? Are they safe from an escaped patient?* "He's still on the loose?" I asked.

"Nah, police caught the guy after a few hours. I wish I

could of seen that driver's face though."

"Me too." I tried to think how someone could get their arms out of that thing and drew a blank. *I sure hope someone recognizes this Houdini if he ever comes to PER.*

Kavon continued on as if he could read my thoughts. "He was probably the same guy that climbed up on the cafeteria roof a couple years back." My eyes bulged. The canvas awning around the cafeteria didn't look like it could support a grown man's weight.

"Don't worry, he was okay. They got him too, as soon as he jumped off on the other side."

As I headed for my car after the shift, I kept looking back over my shoulder to see if any more escapees were coming at me from the rooftop.

❊ ❊ ❊

Every morning I begged—well I wouldn't call it begging. I asked imploringly to stay on PER instead of getting sent to PER 2. PER is where the action is, the place where stories are born. PER 2 was like an excessively watered-down version of PER. Let me rephrase that. PER 2 *was* an excessively watered-down version of PER.  Once PER fills up with patients, the calmest ones get sent to the overflow unit-PER 2. Some endearingly call it the 'good behavior' unit. No action. No fun. Even the inpatient units are more engaging.  Not everyone feels the same way about working at PER2.  The team members who weren't brand new loved getting assigned there so they could catch a break from the commotion of PER.

I practically skipped into the breakroom the next morning for the report, stoked for whatever adventures the shift would bring. I left trudging like I was in a funeral procession. I couldn't talk Kavon out of assigning me to PER 2 this time. I racked my little brain trying to think of another way out. *If I get too bored, then I could start banging my head against the wall so that they would send me back to PER-as a patient, but PER nonetheless.*

Pausing in front of the PER 2 door, I tried to plaster a believable smile on my face before going inside. I didn't want to start off on the wrong foot. Besides, smiling in and of itself makes things a bit more bearable.

Inside PER 2, a wall of plexiglass separated the nurse station from the patients just like in PER. The nurse, Destiny, looked even more relaxed than she did in PER. Destiny looked like she could be cast as Snow White with a Southern accent. Many of her male patients were so charmed that they tried to postpone getting discharged as long as they could.

Tall, lanky Dr. Mbari passed through the nurse station on his way to assess patients. He greeted us warmly. After—*Bzzzt*—badging open the door to the patient floor, he turned to Destiny, crossing his index fingers at her, and declared,

"I see the devil! Stay back!"

I fought the urge to say what I was thinking. *Has he lost it? I can take him back to PER.* They both chuckled, stifling my excuse to go back to PER.

"What was that about, Destiny?" I asked.

"Yesterday I offered a patient some milk and he made the sign of the cross at me and yelled, "I see the devil!"

Still confused, I asked myself *how could someone so calm and compassionate come across as a devil?*

She smiled at my befuddled face. "Little did I know, he was lactose intolerant."

*That makes perfect sense.*

"You forgot to tell him about the part where he pulled out a ring and proposed to you," Dr. Mbari called out from the nurse's window.

I looked back at Destiny. "What did you tell him?"

Destiny half smiled. "That I have a boyfriend and I don't want another one."

"Hopefully he kept the receipt," I replied, "Or at least find someone to buy it."

"He wouldn't get much for it, Jay. It was made of toilet paper."

"Clean toilet paper?"

"Isn't it time for you to check the patient's vital signs?"

A few hours later, which actually felt like a few decades later in PER 2, I reluctantly returned from break. The patients either slept or sat watching *Criminal Minds* on the big screen that faced them from the wall behind the tech desk. Jorge sat with the fluorescent vest on, leaning back sideways in the swivel chair so he could watch.

"Jorge, whose idea was this show?" It felt so tempting to turn and watch the show, but I really didn't want to turn my back on them, especially while they learned different ways to kill people.

"While you were on break we just about had a civil war between watching the baseball game or the Bachelorette, so I turned the TV off until we reached a compromise. The compromise happens to be my favorite show."

Eons later, Jorge left for lunch and so I sat alone, staring at the clock, urging it forward so I could take off this ridiculous vest and get out of this place. *Another dull day at P2,* I silently lamented. Destiny stuck her head out of the nurse station window and shouted, interrupting my perfectly justified whining.

"Hey Jay, they need you to bring some patients from PER, they're swamped. Here's the list." She handed me a scrap of paper with some names scribbled on it. "I'll take the vest so you can go."

I tossed it to her. "All yours."

Bursting through the door, I leapt outside, and paused to savor a deep breath. The stagnant PER 2 air cleared from my lungs. "Ahhhh." Just to feel the sunshine again felt like a treat. A pang of guilt struck and I tried not to think about the patients still stuck inside.

I moseyed into the PER hallway that connected the breakroom and female property storage. Before swinging open the storage door, I paused to prepare myself mentally for the stench that always ensued. *Bzzzt.* Holding the list of names, I checked the tags on the patients' locked blue boxes. They contained whatever the patients had come in with, or rather whatever they came in with that they didn't sneak past us. As I came out of the closet, literally not figuratively, I just about bumped into Susan and tripped over the mop bucket she was pushing. You couldn't miss her between her bubbly personality and her hair's 80's metal band personality. Except for today, that is. I hardly recognized the horrified face in front of me. She looked shell-shocked.

"Whoa there Susan, you're covering for Jordan?" I greeted, wondering what I could say to help her feel better. "That's nice of you to help the custodians do the mopping," I continued.

She took a deep breath. "It's not really an option, Jay. Every seat is taken and we're down two bathrooms and we got a line waiting in triage."

"Two bathrooms?"

"Yeah, we got this lady that won't stop drinking milk."

"If that's the worst thing they do, they can come over to PER 2."

"*Psh*, I wish. She goes so often that she'd have to poop in the courtyard on the way over to PER 2. I've mopped the bathrooms four times. *Four times*, Jay. Her bowels are an active volcano. Each time she comes out of the bathroom, she tells us how she's lactose intolerant and then grabs more milk and I take them away. Every time I start cleaning she goes behind my back and asks someone else, someone who we haven't warned yet and they give her more milk and then she bombs more bathrooms." She shuddered. "I'm gonna sit down now."

"You look pretty shook up, anything else goin' on?" Susan looked me square in the eye.

"Before today, I never had to mop walls before."

It took a minute for me to realize what she meant. I no

longer missed PER. I was torn between disgust and curiosity. *How could anyone's bowels do that?*

The next day, the entire unit sat stewing in their hangriness. I glanced imploringly at the clock. Clamors of "What's for dinner?", "I'm hungry!", and "I haven't ate in 40 days," echoed around the room.

*How much longer until this place combusts into a riot?* I wondered. Punctuating the crescendo of cries, the double doors burst open as a stainless steel box rammed through them and rolled straight toward me. It was just large enough to hide Kavon as he pushed it through. That doesn't mean very tall. I shall forgo commenting on the width.

I breathed a deep sigh of relief. Dinner had arrived. When I placed a hand on the steel door, I didn't want to let it go. It felt so warm, so secure. The box on wheels contained enough to-go boxes for every patient inside PER. That is, every patient that didn't arrive after Kavon did a headcount and ran to the cafeteria.

A nurse, Latricia, stepped out onto the patient floor. "You got six newcomers in triage, Kavon."

Kavon palmed his face.

"Don't worry, I'm caught up so I'll help pass out dinner while you go get more."

Kavon half smiled. "Well thanks, that's awfully kind of you, Latricia."

"Don't get used to it."

Kavon just shook his head and went back out.

I loved passing out the warm to-go boxes and seeing the patient's eye light up, their faces cracking into rare smiles. As every mouth munched away, our ears heard a strange sound. Silence. No yelling, no swearing, no flirting.

*Ah, if only it were mealtime all day.* I thought to myself. *Actually, that would get incredibly messy. Never mind.*

As I finished passing out milk cartons, a middle-aged man, AJ, walked up and grabbed another. His curly black twists of hair framed his deep brown face.

"You mind if I take two more? I don't get milk very often-"

I grinned and nodded, happy to oblige.

"—cause I'm lactose intolerant."

My smile stiffened and my eyes bugged out as I pictured Susan's traumatized face from yesterday. Even if I was interested in cleaning poop off walls, we didn't have time to spare. No way was I going to let that happen.

"Hey! You're lactose intolerant? Then don't drink it!" I retorted.

AJ had already popped one open. "Whadda ya mean don't drink it? You already gave me one," he countered.

"We'll get you some water or something else, just put it back."

"No thanks, I'm good with milk."

"I said put it back." I reached for it, but he spun away and headed down the dimly lit front row to the female side. I childishly chased him.

"What's goin' on?" Kenisha queried.

"I'm not bothering nobody, I'm just tryin' to drink my milk in peace," AJ replied.

I glared at him. "He's lactose intolerant and he's chugging milk. Weren't you here with Susan yesterday?"

Kenisha's eyes scrunched as she tried to block out the memory. "Aw hell no, we're not goin' through that again. Put it down, man."

AJ set a now empty carton on the desk and wiped off a milk mustache with the hand clutching his other carton of milk. "It's a free country, sis."

"Give it back!" I snapped, lunging, snatching the carton out of his hand like a toddler at the playground.

"Hey, man, I'm just trying to drink milk, what's your problem?"

Latricia came out of the nurse station. "What's goin' on here?"

AJ stammered "He took that milk outta my hands, all I

want is some milk. I'm not bothering anybody." He raised his eyebrows, pleading her to advocate for him so he could have more diarrhea.

"I won't let him drink milk 'cause he's lactose intolerant and I don't want to be mopping turds off the walls." I had to put it in context so she knew the consequences of giving him more milk.

"Okay then." Latricia smirked and walked away.

AJ turned back to Kenisha. "I just don't get it, why can't a man just mind his own business and drink milk?"

"A man can, unless his business ends up covering the bathroom walls," Kenisha retorted.

Latricia strode back over to AJ. "Here you go." She gave him not one but two cartons of milk.

"Aw thank you, Miss." He beamed like it was Christmas Day.

I cringed. It felt like Latricia had just sucker-punched me in the stomach. AJ popped the carton open as I turned to Latricia, dumbfounded by her treachery.

"Why'd you do that?"

"It's just milk." Her smirk never left her face as she turned and stepped back inside the nurse station.

"She don't care 'cause she don't have to clean it up," Kenisha grumbled.

Simmering in frustration, I turned back to the triumphant milkman.

"If you miss the toilet, *you* get to mop it up." I waited to hear some sassy reply but he was too busy glugging down another carton.

As we got ready for shift change, I checked the bathrooms. If we left the night shift team with a crusty surprise then we'd never hear the end of it. I badged the door open—*Bzzzt*, flipped light switch—*Click.* I stuck my head and scanned the floors, the walls, even the ceiling.

"Clean! What a nice surprise."

*Bzzzt. Click.* "Clean!"

*Bzzzt. Click.*"Clean?" I reached the final door—*Bzzzt*—and flipped on the light. What I saw left me speechless.  Wall to wall it was covered in... ....spotless tile. I shook my head. This evening, my reaction to AJ made me the craziest one in the room.

# CHAPTER 6: **APRIL SHOWERS...**

The next day I returned from break and went to tell Chris it was his turn to go. He sat stewing at the female side desk. Kavon, wearing the hideously fluorescent vest, stood by his side. They exchanged grumbles. I couldn't tell whose face looked more embittered. They both had that look of an infant who, for the first time in their life, just licked a lemon. I didn't get it, we had no one waiting in line for skin checks, nobody pacing around trying to fight each other, no one competing for who could yell the loudest. It was their dream shift.

"Hey guys, what's up?"

They both turned to me, eyes narrowed.

Kavon nodded toward the video feed from the waiting room cameras. "We just seen who's coming." he then hesitated, as if pronouncing just the name itself tasted bitter. "April."

I waited for them to expound, but they didn't. I threw up my hands in exasperation. "...and?" When they didn't answer, I took a look at the screen.

A petite female with a pixie haircut and peachy hue sat merrily munching on a bag of Doritos. I expect a commission for that, Frito Lay. "You're scared of this tiny lady who's minding her own business?"

"You'll see," Kavon muttered.

"But you'll hear her first," Chris grumbled.

On either side of her sat yeti-sized police officers. From the look on their faces, they both sat there wondering, "Why did I choose this profession? Why?"

"You see those chips," Kavon asked.

"Yeah, they're just chips," I replied.

"I gave those to her as a peace offering, but I'm tellin' ya, as soon as she swallows the last one the ceasefire is over." April began licking the Dorito dust from her fingers as the officers led her over to the triage room.

I knew Kavon bribed patients, but I'd never seen him go to the waiting room to do it. *This has to be a prank*, I told myself. Just then, shrill screams reverberated through triage.

"I DON'T WANNA BE HERE, I DO NOT CONSENT, #%&@*S!"

Jackie stepped out of triage and closed the door behind her, staring grimly at the ground. I'd never seen her like that. She power walked up to Kavon. *Is she in on the prank too?*

"I called the other units, they're sending Deante and Jack over. Oh, and she's gonna need a poncho." I tried to fit these new pieces into the puzzle. *That means there's some skin that needs to get covered up. This is just too weird to be a prank.*

Kavon sighed. "Chris, grab a poncho and let's get this over with."

"You gonna say, 'Please?'" Chris retorted.

"GIVE ME THAT #%&@ING PHONE I HAVE THE RIGHT TO CALL MY #%&@ING LAWYER!" resounded from triage.

Kavon rolled his eyes. "Chris, this ain't the time for that, just grab the poncho, and let's go."

Chris grumbled and grabbed a poncho. He, Jack, and Jorge clustered around Kavon, who stood at the triage door, peeking in through the little window. Kavon took a deep breath, swung open the door, and stepped inside.

"WHO'S THIS SON OF A #%&@?"

"This son of a #%&@ is the PER floor supervisor," he replied. I could hear Kavon's smirk.

"SO WHAT?"

"It's dinner time."

"THE FOOD HERE #%&@ING SU—"

"We got a quiet room open if ya want it," Kavon whispered.

"—CKS. Wait, what?"

"I said, 'We got a quiet room available.' I know you're hungry and tired. I was gonna go bring dinner to everybody, but there's too much commotion goin' on over here, so I can't go no more."

Not a peep from April.

Kavon continued. "If it gets quiet in here we can take off those handcuffs and get you in that room so you can get some rest."

"Okay." I heard the click of the handcuff key. As she stepped through the door and into the unit, she whipped around. "There better not be any restraints in there."

Kavon gazed up at the ceiling. I could hear his thoughts, "Lord have mercy. Please." He looked her in the eye. "We didn't put no restraints in there, and we'll keep it that way as long as you keep it together. Jorge, are there any restraints in there?"

"No."

"Okay, I'll go." April retorted. "But you're gonna get hell if there is."

"Right this way, Miss." Jorge placed a hand on her elbow.

She shook her elbow, stomped, and glared up at him. "I'm goin' by myself." When she reached the door she peered around for restraints before entering. "Are these sheets clean?"

"Yeah, I just barely put them on," Jorge muttered

"Okay, well, you go grab dinner and I'll be waiting here." Jorge bit his tongue as he closed the door.

The next morning, Jorge and I arrived in the breakroom to find a tall, stoic guy with short black, coily hair. His tan scrubs told us he was a team supervisor. He leaned against the refrigerator with his copper-toned arms folded.

"You must be the new guys on Kavon's team. I'm Trey." He extended a fist in greeting. Like Kavon, he was down to earth despite his position. After our introduction, Trey pulled out his phone, checked the time, then shook his head. The door opened and in came Jordan.

"Jordan, you're never late. What happened?" Trey asked.

"I don't know what you're talking about, I clocked in on time," she told him.

"Well, one experienced person's here. I have no idea when Chris or Kavon are gonna show up, so I'm giving report now." He cracked open the worn monitor binder and pointed at the male side pictures.

"This guy, Robby, in 3B just got here. He's been chill but I'm not sure if he'll stay like that. The rest of that row just slept and ate. Here in 2A you got Martin. He didn't get along with Gerard in 6B so we moved him over there. Nothing physical, just a lot of smack-talking when everybody else wants to sleep. On the female side, these three are quiet and shocked to be here so hopefully they'll get transferred to PER 2 after shift change. The other ones just slept. As for the quiet rooms, the male side is now empty. They just went in-patient so you lucked out there, but I apologize. April is still here. She was the same as usual."

"No surprise there," Jordan muttered.

Chris and Kavon came through the door, each holding a drink.

"Oh hey there Trey, you have a good shift?" Kavon asked.

Trey shook his head. "Let's just say I'm glad I'm going home. I already gave report and I'm not repeating myself so you're gonna have to ask the rest of your squad here. Good luck with April."

Kavon's brow furrowed. "She didn't go in-patient yet?"

Trey grinned. "Good luck." He turned to Jorge and I. "Nice to meet you two. See ya'll in twelve hours." He handed me the binder and walked out.

As I made my rounds in the atrocious vest, I peeked inside the quiet room. There was April, wrapped up in a nest of blankets. Her dinner tray sat open on the floor surrounded by a few open cartons of milk. We passed out breakfast, sausage and biscuits, but she still snoozed away. Not daring to wake her, Chris opened her door and set a steaming hot tray on the floor with a couple of milk cartons.

I ambled down the space behind the male rows, stifling a yawn as I marked off where each patient was and what they did..

74

*3B Kyle sleeping, 4B Colton bathroom, 5B Brock sleeping.* When I looked up from the binder, I met the gaze of the tall, wiry old man from 6B, leering into my face from where he stood on top of his recliner.  He towered over me, dark brown brow furrowed with irritation, eyes wide with conviction.

"I AM THE CREATOR," he boomed, "I WILL SMITE YOU."

I took a couple steps back and his fiery wrath simmered. His neighbor in 7B let out a snore, oblivious to the presence of this deity. If he could sleep through that, he must come here quite a bit. He probably needed it. The people that lived in the street usually went right to sleep. It's hard to sleep if you have to keep warm, find food, and keep your belongings from getting stolen all at the same time.

The next time I rounded; 6B, Raymond, told me that he was the president and had on a bulletproof vest. I felt disappointed. I still  had quite a few questions for the Creator and several requests.  I nodded my understanding and continued accounting for patients. It wouldn't be the last time I met with a deity. At least he was much nicer as a president than he was as a deity.

Back inside the nurse's station, I recounted the characters from 6B to Jackie, the ginger charge nurse. She casually downed the last drops of her frappuccino.

"Well Jay, that's just Raymond.  Last time he was John the Baptist. I guess he got a promotion."


When it came time for lunch, Kavon left to go get the cart. Right after the doors closed behind him, April's door cracked open and a ball of blankets with legs stepped out.   The ball yawned and then a human face poked out.

"I'm starving and the milk in my room is warm and the breakfast is cold. You got something that's actually edible?" April shouted.

"Actually, lunch will be here in a minute. Kavon just left to pick it up," I offered.

"If you were starving you would have eaten it," Chris

muttered under his breath.

"I want a hot *breakfast*," she replied.

"I'm sorry, it's all cold, but lunch will be hot," I replied.

She stepped toward me. "You're not getting it. Not cold. Not lunch. Hot breakfast. Do I need to spell it out for you?"

Chris folded his burly arms. "April, when you were sleeping we were nice enough not to wake you up. I left your hot breakfast in your room. You slept in late so it's cold now. You'll have to wait."

"Well, can I at least get another blanket?"

Pursing his lips, Chris went to the linen cart and pulled out a blanket as she went back into her room, shutting the door behind her.

"Hey, you said you wanted a blanket."

"I do," came the muffled reply.

Brow furrowed, he swung open her door and tossed it onto the bed.

"Here's your blanket, just remember, you're not at a hotel."

"I'm still hungry." She picked up an open milk carton in each hand.

"You're gonna get sick if you drink that," he told her. "Just stay in here and we'll bring you lunch."

"DON'T TELL ME WHAT TO DO!"

He couldn't help himself. "So it's okay for you to tell everybody else what to do, but not the other way around?"

She stood up and flung both her arms at him, dousing him in milk.

As it splattered off him, Chris stepped backward, squeezing his eyes shut, convincing himself not to explode. "You're a grown woman. Don't expect nothing from us if you're gonna act like that," he boomed. He stepped out and closed the door.

"I SAID DON'T TELL ME WHAT TO DO, #%&@!"

Chris stared back at me as milk dripped from his curls and onto his already-soaked scrubs. He shook his head. "It's not worth it. I'm gonna go change." As he reached for the break room door, I heard him mutter, "Me and my big mouth."

I was just impressed that he didn't deck her.

After Chris had showered, changed, and returned, Kavon tossed him the vest.

"How was the spa?"

One of Chris's eyebrows sprung up. "Say what?"

"How was the spa? You been gone for an hour."

Chris shook his head. "At least one of us has to look good, Kavon."

Kavon grinned. "Don't fool yourself, Chris. You'd better go get a refund if you was trying to look as good as me."

Chris smiled for the first time today and began his rounds in the hideous vest. When the dinner cart arrived, Chris was nice enough to help us pass it out. The sooner everyone gets their trays, the sooner they leave everybody else alone. Chris bravely set a plate in the entryway of April's lair.

A few minutes later, her door creaked open, and she poked her head out. "Hey, you got the meal, but where's the milk? I'm parched."

Chris glowered. "Why would I get you more milk if you just threw it all over me? You're not getting anymore."

"I hope you get fired." She slammed the door.

"Me too, then I wouldn't have to deal with you," he muttered under his breath.

The patients lay in their recliners, sedated from the hot meal, all except for Kevin, a spindly, soft-spoken young man with black hair and cream skin tone.

"Hey, can I take a shower?"

"Sure." Then I saw he had on a blue wristband, which meant we couldn't let him go alone behind a closed door because he might harm himself.

"Let me get you some towels, but just heads up, I gotta have my foot in the door.

"Yeah, it's okay. I really need a shower."

As I stood there with my foot in the door, facing out towards the patient floor, I pretended it wasn't as awkward as it really is. I marveled at how quiet it had gotten. *Amazing what a hot meal can do.*

As Kevin waited for the water to get hot, he began singing a Taylor Swift song. I'm not going to critique his singing. Let's just say that everyone was fortunate that he didn't sing very loudly. Meanwhile, Kavon plodded between the rows in the vest, marking down where each patient was at. As he reached the quiet room, April poked her head out.

"Hey, I want my shoes please."

"I'm sorry, April, you know we can't do that here. Is there something else we can do for you?"

"I said I want my shoes, PLEASE!"

"Look, we can give you some of our flip-flops so you're not stepping on the floor, I can get you some socks to keep your feet warm, but I can't get your stuff outta your box until you're discharged. She grimaced but said nothing. Kavon moved on to check on the front row of the female side.

"I SAID GIVE ME MY SHOES, #%&@*R," she snarled from behind him. She began power walking toward him.

Kavon glanced up from his notes. His right eyebrow twitched, the only sign that she had gotten to him. "Look, do you see any other patients here with shoes on? I know you want your shoes but that's a big safety issue. Is there something else I can do for you?"

"Well, #$%@ YOUR#%&@ING RULES!"

Kavon held her gaze without blinking.

I turned and yelled into the crack of the bathroom door, "Kevin! Hurry up! We got a situation on our hands."

"Okay!" Kevin shouted before bursting back into another Taylor Swift song.

"Shake it off! Just shake it off!"

*Stop shaking and get out of the shower!* I wanted to scream.

April turned to go back to her room. Kavon began scribbling notes again as he walked further down the row. After he took a couple steps away, April turned around and rushed at him.

"KAVON, WATCH OUT!" I shouted.

He turned just in time to dodge a haymaker. "Woah, there, was that just for the shoes?"

"CODE GREEN, PER," echoed over the intercom.

April wagged a finger under his nose.

"You #%&@*s don't give a #%&@ about anybody, do you? Well, I've HAD IT WITH THIS #%&@!" Without warning, she launched another haymaker at his head. He slipped it, and she swung again. Kavon bobbed and weaved with uncharacteristic speed. I squirmed, wanting to watch and wanting to turn away at the same time. Reinforcements hadn't arrived, I was still stuck at this door, and I wasn't sure how long he could keep dodging.

"YOU COWARD!" She rushed at him again, cocking her fist as the nurse station door crashed open from behind her. A streak of fluorescent green jolted behind her, and Chris bear-hugged her, grabbing both her wrists. Darius would be proud.

"That's enough April," he scolded.

"You get your #%&@ING hands offa me, #%&@!"

Streams of green scrubs poured in through both double doors, sweeping April up and back into her room. Dee followed with two syringes and before we knew it, April began serenading us with snores.


The following morning, I walked into the breakroom to find Chris chatting with a slim, tall guy whose afro made him look even more tall and slim than he already was.

"Hey, these must be the new guys you were talkin' about." He extended a hand and smiled. "I'm Zion." After pointing out what quirks we should watch out for in the patients, he paused. "I heard what happened yesterday and I hate to break it to you but April's still here. Please be careful out there. Now, who's taking the vest first?"

Jordan raised her hand.

"Alright, well here you go. I'm off to class."

I can't imagine going to class after a twelve-hour night shift. He and Chris were studying for their Master's Degrees. It's hard to make a living off a Bachelor's in Psychology.

A few hours later, I sat at the female side desk, entering results into the computer. Chris rounded the quiet rooms in the ugly vest.

Destiny strode up to me with a pack of papers. She slapped them onto the desk, declaring, "Finally. April's ready for discharge."

Chris turned and perked up.

"Okay, I'll take care of it after I finish putting these results in," I replied.

"Jay, how about taking care of those results after you take her out before she stirs up more trouble," Chris interjected.

"Take her out? As in to dinner? That's unethical."

"Jay, it's too early for dad jokes."

April patiently stood in front of the female side desk as I plopped her tiny property tub on the desk. She wore the smallest size of paper scrubs, yet the pants were so big on her that it looked as if she was entering a sack race.

"Alright, April, let me get out your clothes  so you can change, I'll cut off your wristband and then I'll show you where the bus stop is."

"Sounds good. I'm sick of these paper scrubs."

I popped the zip ties off her little box to find a pair of old flip-flops and a black apron. I raised an eyebrow. "Did you come in with anything else?"

"No, that's all I was wearing when the police came picked me up."

"Okay, I'll run grab some clothes for you to wear under it."

"No, I'll just wear this. I want to wear it."

"We can't do that. It's cold out there." I tried not to imagine the situation where some poor soul crossed her on the crosswalk, thinking she had on shorts and a tank top underneath and then realizing she didn't when they passed by each other. I was torn between laughing and throwing up. Fortunately, the two reactions canceled each other out so I could keep a straight face. Don't worry, dear reader, I didn't let her leave until she had on a pair of jeans and a T-Shirt from the donation closet. *Bzzzt*—we left the courtyard and entered the front of the building. As I waved hello to the receptionist, Ms. Griffin, "Code Green Unit 3" echoed over the intercom. I froze, silently cursing my luck. As much as I wanted to, I couldn't just leave April here. Thanks to Peaceful Pines policy, I had to escort her off the premises, all the way on the other side of the parking lot. I began speed walking, hoping she would follow suit.

"The bus stop is gonna be around the corner there-"

"Yeah, I know, I've been in and outta here plenty of times."

"Well, hope your day gets better from here."

"Thanks. Catch ya next time."

As soon as she stepped off the parking lot pavement, I turned around and dashed to the front door. I didn't want to miss any more codes. I especially didn't want to get any idea about what she chose to wear or not wear off the premises.

# CHAPTER 7: **IMPOSTERS**

The next morning I felt so good, I almost whistled as I stepped out of my battered, old sedan and made my way to the breakroom to get report. I say almost because I don't know how to whistle. I couldn't wait to see what stories would come from today's shift. I beamed as I swung open the break room door. The breakroom was lifeless.

Ruby from night shift sat with the binder open in her lap, her head hanging down in slumber. She had shoulder length curly black hair and a deep brown complexion. She was twice my size and her personality was twice her size. I didn't want to startle her awake, so I decided to keep quiet until the rest of day shift got here.

"You're not even goin' to say good morning? That's a terrible way to start your shift," she said, almost making me jump in surprise.

Only then did I notice her phone tucked in the binder as she looked back down and began scrolling away.

*Was she really awake the whole time or was she just trying to save face?* I wondered to myself. "G-good morning." *Stupid stutter.*

"That's more like it, sunshine. Where's the rest of your crew? I gotta go get some breakfast."

"They're on their way." For all I knew they were stuck in traffic or still home sleeping or being devoured by bears. I chose to give them, and the bears, the benefit of the doubt.

"Wassup, Ruby?" Kavon came in and held out a fist.

She slowly bumped it with hers. "Pretty much falling asleep here waiting for you to show up, that's wassup. I swear I got cobwebs hangin' off me."

"Well Jay and I are here, why don't you give us the run down and we'll tell the others when they get here?"

"That's fine with me. It was a really quiet night until Betty came in. She's in 1A so it's easier to keep an eye on her. As for the others," she began pointing at their pictures, "slept all night, slept, slept, slept, got some snacks and slept, yeah nothing else really. Bernardo, this good lookin' guy in 1B got brought in a few hours ago. He just speaks Spanish so no one really knows what's goin' on with him. The police said something about him wanting to hurt himself so he got a blue band on."

Jordan, who had arrived just in time to hear the part about a good-looking guy, leaned in to get a good look at the picture. "I'll take the vital signs on the male side as soon as we're done here," she volunteered.

"You better start learning Spanish then," Ruby cut in. "Now the quiet rooms are all empty, and this is Jeremy," Ruby held up a picture of a young, lanky, red-headed guy in a poncho.

"He just got here so we don't have a seat for him yet. It's seven AM and I'm off."

Kavon stood up as she left. "Alright, Jay you take vitals on the male side, Jordan you get the female side, Chris get the vest and I'll do the rest."

"Did you not hear me? I got the male side," Jordan replied.

"Jay speaks Spanish. Do you?"

Jordan rolled her eyes.

"I'll take that as a no. You can get afternoon vitals after we know what's up with him."

*"SCREEeeeEEE."* The squeaky cart sounded worse than my thirteen-year-old brother in the middle of puberty. *"Please don't wake anyone up,"* I groaned as I dragged it to row B. Bernardo looked up with big  sad eyes and took a deep breath which probably meant 'Not another gringo who doesn't know Spanish.'

"Buenos días, Bernardo. ¿Me permites tomar tus signos vitales?" I asked, which means, "Good morning, Bernardo. Can you take your vital signs?".

His forlorn face cracked into a great grin as he perked up in the recliner. His white teeth seemed to shine in the dim room.

"Claro que sí."

He held out a massive arm. As I wrapped the blood pressure cuff around it, he poured out what he'd been holding in the whole night.

"Man, I'm so, so glad you're here. I got here and tried explaining my situation but nobody understood me, they just gave me a snack and a blanket. I'm not suicidal or anything like that, it's just a big misunderstanding. You see, I was taking the bus from Miami to go to my cousin's place in Chicago but I missed a connection. I just came here from Cuba so I couldn't make sense of all the signs. I had no idea where I was on the route. I didn't know anyone, in fact, no one around me even spoke my language. Hours went by as I waited at the stop with no way to get ahold of my cousin and no way to get back. The police saw me crying and said I was suicidal and took me here." His voice cracked, "I don't even know what city this is."

Confused, I wondered why no one had used the language interpretation line. It's required, but the language lines don't always have decent connection.

"Let me tell them what really happened and we'll see what we can do."

I explained the situation to the social worker, Jamie, who made a few calls to verify his story.

"Hey Jay, I'm gonna take break, you cover the desk," Kavon boomed.

"Got it." A grizzled old man sat slumped in the chair beside the desk, waiting to get checked in. The chairs accessible to patients were weighted to prevent any budding professional wrestlers from wielding them as a weapon. This man appeared too tired to pick up even a regular dining room chair.

As I sat down at the desk, I met Bernardo's questioning gaze.

"Don't worry, I told 'em. Now all we can do is wait."

He nodded. "That's more information than I've gotten all night. Thank you."

"Of course. I'll let you know when we get any updates."

"Again, thank you, really."

I looked down, unsure of how to answer. No one had expressed so much gratitude before. I folded open the computer shell attached to the wall and logged in to the computer so I could check in the newcomers.

"You got a picture for the binder?" Jordan, wearing the hideous vest, approached the male side desk. She glanced more than once at Bernardo.

"No, I'm just about to do that."

The newcomer's stench, matted hair and tattered clothes held untold stories of hardship. I tried to make a habit of introducing myself to patients as if this was any other professional establishment. They seemed to appreciate it. Tall and gangly, young Jeremy walked by and paused in front of the desk. His blue eyes bulged from his ginger face as he looked me in the eye.

"#%&@ you, Jay." He then continued his lap around the rows of recliners.

"Good morning to you, too, Jeremy."

I mean they seemed to appreciate it except for him. When I introduced myself and shook the old man's hand, he sat up and seemed to glow. That's what I loved about this job.

Kavon strolled up to the desk. "You workin' hard, got great customer service and people are noticing, baby boy." Kavon good-naturedly slapped me on the shoulder. I had made it through the first two weeks without snapping. As Kavon escorted the exhausted man for his skin check, I turned to see a long line of men of every conceivable shape, color, and demeanor sitting along the wall, waiting to get checked in. *They could have anything in their pockets,* I told myself. *If we don't get everyone checked in quickly then we're asking for a riot.* I beckoned for the next guy in line. The slender fellow stared at me and sashayed over with such swagger it seemed he thought he was modeling on a runaway rather than a dimly-lit psychiatric unit.

He placed a hand on one hip and waved the other in my face.

"You have five minutes to impress me."

I just stared back, considering the repercussions of what I wanted to say: *I'm hungry and there's a massive line. It's going to be a long five minutes for you.* Finally, I responded, "There's not enough room to breakdance," and got back to work. He wasn't impressed by my data-entering skills. If he really wanted to be impressed, then he should have gone to Disneyland instead of Peaceful Pines. So much for my customer service skills.

Eventually, I glanced back at the line of newcomers. *Just two left and I can breathe again,* I reassured myself. Then *Cory* came down from triage. I took a deep breath. Some patients come back so often that you have their quirks, triggers, and motives memorized. Cory left an unforgettable impression. The first time I saw him come in, my body tensed, ready for a fight. I kept him in sight the whole time, trying to anticipate when he would explode. While the average patient kept to themselves and acted normally, Cory acted like a stereotypical psychiatric patient. I soon became accustomed to seeing the short, stocky fellow twitching, swearing, and punching at thin air. His chart said something about schizophrenia, but he had one of the most animated cases of schizophrenia I've ever seen. His rough demeanor and odor suggested that he spent most of his time in the street. Fortunately for now, he sat a few chairs down from the desk, so his stench was tolerable. As Cory waited his turn, he stood. Bristling, he turned toward the wall and squared off as if to fight, shouting threats peppered with words that I will not repeat.

"Did you see that?" he asked me, pointing a tan finger at the wall in front of him.

"See what?" I saw nothing more than a wall.

When it was his turn to get checked in, he plopped down

in the chair while I set up his paperwork. Nurses and supervisors bustled about, paying no heed to his tirades and twitches. When there came a lull in the commotion—when all my coworkers were on the other side of the unit—Cory looked over his shoulder. He abruptly stopped twitching and cursing the air. It seemed as if someone flipped a switch off. Then he turned to me.

"Hey, I remember you. You're a pretty cool guy. How you been?"

He had some level of illness, but apparently, he played it up in order to get a meal and a place to spend the night. It became difficult to trust patients after that, but eventually, I learned to roll with it. You have to take people seriously if you want to communicate with them. Focusing on skepticism just sets one up for failure and misery.

Once we had gotten all the men checked in, I began wiping off the desk with disinfectant. I hardly paid attention to the calm conversations around me until...

"Yeah, you know I'm a green beret."

I paused and looked up, searching for a massive, muscular he-man. It took me a minute to realize that the self-proclaimed green beret was a short, chubby fellow with a peachy babyface talking at a couple of men over by the patient phones. Usually, I try to give people the benefit of the doubt, but my imagination wasn't flexible enough for this. I wondered why anyone would say that. *PER is a scary place, so maybe he thinks that his hyperbole would keep him safe.*

Kavon hustled over. "Those guys over there are gettin' discharged. I'll grab their stuff while you check them out."

"But I don't find them attractive."

"Say what?"

I grabbed their files. "Never mind." Not everyone appreciates a good dad joke.

One by one, I started verifying their name bracelets with their files before popping open the zip-tied boxes and giving them their belongings back. Kavon would then escort them to the bathroom so they could change back into their street clothes.

"Alright, Lyle, come on up, I got your box here." A middle-aged man in blue paper scrubs trudged up to the desk.

"I'll just have you verify the zip-tie numbers with your property sheet and you can sign and I'll pop it open." As he scribbled a signature, I popped open the little box to take out his clothes. As soon as I looked inside, my brow contorted in confusion. There was nothing more than a package of cigarettes and a bus pass.

"Where's your clothes?"

"I don't have none."

*Obviously, you're just wearing paper scrubs,* I thought to myself. "I mean before they brought you in here."

"I *said*, I don't have no clothes." His eyes narrowed in irritation.

I felt even more confused than before. "What do you mean, you didn't come in with no clothes?"

As he glared at me, it dawned on me that not everyone comes into Peaceful Pines fully dressed. Some came transferred by ambulance in hospital gowns. Others came in whatever the police could cover them with because they had been running around in their birthday suits. For once, I had the intelligence not to delve any deeper.

"Okay, well, I'll go run to the donation closet and see if I can find some clothes for you. What size are you?"

A set of clothes later, everyone was ready, so I began cutting off their wristbands. The tall, lanky white guy from 2B held out his wrist.

"Nice try, Will" He wasn't on the list.

Will grinned mischievously. "I can't wait to get out of here, man. I could be earning all sorts of money right now."

"Oh yeah," I asked, "what would you be doing?"

"Oh, I'd be panhandling by the I-6 underpass."

*You call that earning money?* I caught myself before I said it. "Really. How much do you make doing that?"

"Well, on a typical day if I do eight hours I get around

190$."

I frowned as my mood plummeted. That was more than I made in a 12-hour shift! It felt as if he had just punched me in the liver. Trying to maintain my composure, I asked myself *what am I doing with my life?* For a split second, the urge surged within me to rip off my badge and run to the I-6 underpass.

I love escorting discharged patients out as long as I'm not thinking about my meager paycheck. They grin in anticipation when I cut their ID band off as if it were a shackle coming off. As soon as they step out of the double doors and into the lush courtyard, you can see the tension release from their face. At ease, they open up about their life back home. I get a better look at who they are beyond the handcuffs, locked doors, and severed ties to the outside world. They have the same hopes and dreams as anyone else. What would you look forward to if you were about to get discharged after a couple nights in this place? So far, everything patients told me along the walk out was G-rated.

"I can't wait to see my dog, I've been worried sick about him."

"I miss my kids, I'm going to hug them so much."

"I'm ready to get back with my volleyball team. We're like a family."

"The first thing I'm gonna do is go to Whataburger and stuff myself. I'm ready to eat whatever I want."

Yes, I'm waiting for a commission from Whataburger too. *Bzzt*—I let the line of patients into the breezeway and paused, making sure the door shut and that no one had snuck in before —*Bzzzt*—opening the door to outside. As I led them out, I waited for an opening to chat, but the self-proclaimed green beret, Carl, would *not* stop talking. I heard that to qualify for special forces, one must swim underwater for 50 meters. He might actually be able to do that based on how much he could talk without taking a breath. Even if he did look like a green beret, he would have been captured in no time because he could not keep quiet at all.

"Last time I came here, I got fed up and almost walked

out," Carl told the guy next to him. "It took six of them guys in the green scrubs to hold me down." I fought the temptation to single-handedly put him in a hold and prove him wrong. The other patient just nodded his head. We both wondered why the doctors would discharge him in this state.

When we got to the waiting room, Carl's mom wrapped him up in her big arms. He didn't resist. Seeing people reunite with their families is the best. I realized that he had a connection with his mother just like I did. Was he really that different from me?

By lunch, Jamie, the social worker, had a Greyhound voucher in hand for Bernardo's bus ride to Chicago. When I told him, he beamed.

"Thank you so, so much. I would have been stuck here if it weren't for you." I knew he would have gotten out in a matter of days, but I just nodded. Bernardo seemed so happy and I didn't want to interrupt the moment. It's not like I'm the only Spanish speaker in this place. Bernardo grabbed my hand. Usually, I would have jerked it away, but I was dumbfounded by his gratitude.

"I'll never forget you or what you did for me." He was gone by the time I wondered why I didn't give Jamie any credit. She did all the heavy lifting.

The dim lighting of the crisis unit was calming for the patients, even romantic for some. But for the employees, it was depressing. I looked forward to accompanying people to other units because we got to walk through the open-air courtyard of the hospital. This time, I escorted a well-insulated elderly lady from the crisis stabilization unit to an inpatient unit. The yellow bracelet on her cream colored wrist announced to the world that we considered her a fall risk, which is why I kept within arms reach. As she shuffled along with her walker, I grinned, smiling at the warm sunshine I had yearned for while inside the low light of the PER unit. I carried her belongings in a sealed blue tub under one arm, keeping the other ready in case she stumbled.

"What do you miss most about home, Janice?"

"My dog, Brownie. Oh, I miss her dearly. A lot of people won't let their dog on the couch, but I love it when she climbs up next to me and snuggles up with her head on my lap. Then she scoots her wet nose under my hand until I start scratching between her ears."

"So who's taking care of her while you're away?"

"Fortunately my neighbor is taking care of her. It was such short notice, I wasn't sure what to do."

I nodded, grinning at the refreshing cool summer breeze as it playfully rustled through my hair.

Then she stopped the small talk. "I'm going to call you Precious. You're so cute, I could fold you up and put you in my pocket."

She must have misinterpreted that smile. I no longer wanted to be within arm's reach of her. I wrestled with the conundrum of staying out of her reach but close enough to catch her if she took a tumble. *Curse that fall-risk label,* I silently complained. I compromised by holding her box of belongings between us. Fortunately, she didn't try to make any moves. Unfortunately, others would. Taking a patient outside always ran the risk of an escape attempt, but I was confident that I could outrun her, outwalk her, or out crawl her even if she had a 50-foot head start.

After I had dropped her off and stepped back outside, I found the skies had suddenly grayed. Rain poured down, pattering rhythmically on the awning over the sidewalk that connected all the units.

As I made my way back through the drizzle, I saw Damion, a tech, holding the door to Unit Three open so the better-behaved patients could go to the cafeteria for lunch—accompanied by a staff member of course. Among the variety of men and women standing in the doorway, a shock of ginger hair loomed over them and Jeremy's head popped up as soon as he came outside. He had wrapped himself in one of the white ponchos patients get to keep warm. When he felt the raindrops, Jeremy shook his hips and jubilantly leaped into the air as the poncho billowed like a cape.

"It's raining! My rain dance worked!" He exclaimed.

I wondered if he did the rain dance daily until it actually rained. At least he was in a better mood now. *I'm glad he gets to enjoy this fresh air,* I thought to myself. *If I was stuck all day inside the stagnant smell of stale air, I would go insane myself.*

*Two hours left of this shift,* I reassured myself. I dragged the vital sign cart around the male side, going from person to person in a haze brought on by hunger. *At least it's calm.* I pulled the blood pressure cuff off of Robert, the heavy white guy in 4A. Without a word, he rolled over in his recliner and threw the blanket back over his head.

A voice came from behind. "Hi, Jay."

"Oh, hi." It was one of the new social workers, Janet, on her way out to get dinner. I could tell she was new to PER by how happy she looked. Her porcelain skin almost made her glow in the dim lighting. I tried not to feel envious that she got to leave the unit and eat. I moved on to 3A, another mound of blankets. Prepared to duck if he took a swing at me, I tapped the armrest to gently rouse him.

"Hey James, time to check your blood pressure real quick and I'll leave you alone."

A dark arm protruded from the mound of blankets. I put the cuff on and pressed START. The machine groaned, as usual, almost drowning out Janet's heavy footsteps and the typical *"Bzzzt"* as the double doors unlocked. Without looking up, I waited to hear the usual click as they locked. *"CLICK." Good,* I thought, *I don't have to go run to close that door before someone tries to get out.*

"HEY, Jay, GO!" Jordan shouted from the female side.

Jordan's lips trembled and her eyes welled up with worry, in contrast to her usual cool, calm demeanor. I knew something was bad but looking around, all the patients sat still and quiet.

Exasperated by my confusion, she explained "A patient followed Janet into the entryway."

As if on cue, a muffled shout, "GIFFMEEYORBAGE!" came from behind the closed door. I dashed up to the door, held up my badge—*Bzzzt*— and shoved it open before leaping into the breezeway, ready to pounce. As I entered, my eyes met Janet's. Her face had drained of what little color it had. Her eyes wrinkled with worry. Janet stood in front of me, blocking the door leading outside. She clutched her badge in both hands. Parts of her badge clip littered the floor.

"I SAID GIVE ME YOUR BADGE!" blared into my right ear. The words reverberated through the small room. I turned to see a fit, Asian-looking man about my size right next to me. He shook with rage s he glared at Janet

"We can't do that," Janet responded, her voice trembling almost as much as her knees.

"What's going on here?" I asked him. Stupid question, I know, but my rushing adrenaline drowned out what little common sense I had. My MAM training floundered beside it.

"CODE GREEN, PER," echoed over the intercom

"LET ME OUT NOW!"

He turned and kicked the door behind him. It shook. Janet and I stood dumbfounded.

"I SAID NOW!" POW—He punched the door, his fist landing closer to me than the kick had. "NOW!" POW that one landed even closer to me.

I didn't want to find out where the next one would land. Reflexively, I raised my hands, and lunged in, clinching him by the shoulder and collar, and shoved him away from me into the opposite corner. He caught his balance and, glaring me square in the eye, raised his fists.

*Time to raise mine too,* I told myself. Then I realized they were already raised and clenched into fists. He had just followed my cue. I cautiously opened my hands in a gesture of peace but kept them raised to block any punches. His face relaxed and he opened his hands as well. My adrenals simmered down.

"Look man, what's your name?" I asked him.

"Jesse."

"Jesse, I know you don't want to be here, but this isn't helping you. As a—" *Bzzzt*—The unit door swung open and a flood of green poured in between us, led by Chris.

"GET AWAY FROM THEM," Chris barked.

He and Ray each grabbed one of Jesse's arms. I could hardly see Jesse between all the techs packed shoulder to shoulder in the tiny space. *Just when I was getting it under control*, I pouted to myself. *I don't need that much help.* I started feeling claustrophobic, jammed in this tiny room with all these guys in green. Then, like a wave receding from the shore, the flood of green flowed back inside the unit, carrying Jesse along in the current. Stunned, I slowly stepped out behind them. They had already dragged him into the quiet room.

I went back into the breezeway. The color had come back into Janet's face. It wasn't much, because she was extremely pale to begin with.

"Thanks for coming, Jay."

"You're welcome, but I didn't do anything special. How do you feel?"

She let out a deep breath. "A little shaken, but good. Relieved." She bent down to pick up the pieces of her badge clip. "How about you?"

I bent down to help her. "Surprised and pretty stupid for the way I handled it."

"Well, you were the first one in. I didn't know what he was going to try to do to me."

I paused to consider that, like most moments in life, saying the perfect thing didn't matter. Showing up and being present mattered the most.

❈ ❈ ❈

Every shift change between day and night staff leaves windows of opportunity for mischief to spring up before the new team fully adjusts. Unfortunately, I have not mastered quantum tunneling and can only be in one place at a time. So, some necessary tasks like taking vital signs require us to turn our backs to the patients. They may or may not be lying in wait for the right moment to unleash their mischief like a crocodile waiting in a watering hole. Today that mischief came in the form of a spindly white-haired woman. She looked like she had come straight from a retirement community advertisement, including the perm. Unlike most retirees, she would not sit down for more than a millisecond.

Elderly patients raise a new dimension of chaos in the unit. Aside from frailty and risk of falling, they were often the most outspoken pugilists. They either warmed your heart or made  you shudder at the mere mention of their name, like Bertha did. Fortunately, this one was a sweet soul. Unfortunately, we soon learned that every time she walked, she began wobbling as if we were in the middle of an earthquake. It wouldn't be so bad except that she loved to stand and walk as soon as we sat her down. It was as if a magnetic field repelled her from her seat.  Every time I saw Betty's frail frame shakily stand and begin to walk, my heart started quivering more than she already did.  The ones who are least steady on their feet are always the ones who have the greatest gumption for getting going on those wobbly feet. It's better known as Jay's First Law of Peaceful Pines Physics. You better not steal it.

Time and again Betty would teeter over to the male side, grab the blanket off some random snoozing guy and shout, "Wake up! It's time to get up!"

If I had tried that, those fellows would have fed me a fist. Each time they saw this frail figure imposing on their slumber, they chose sympathy over irritation. That impressed me. Patience usually evaporates in the charged setting of PER. Time and again we would redirect her and explain how it could result in bodily harm. It was already the wrong place and the wrong time. There was no telling when she would stumble into the wrong person. After the fifth episode of this, I tried moving her chair to the far corner of the female side, but to no avail.

One large lady chattered away on the phone as casually as if she was home in her kitchen. "Yeah, yeah, he's so handsome but you know what I heard?"

Our obtrusive friend Betty came right up to her and began snatching at her ankles.

Confused, the woman moved her feet out of reach.

"What are you doing, Betty?" I asked, perplexed.

"I'm trying to get that baby," Betty replied. The look on her face said, "Obviously. Are you crazy or what?"

She ended up in restraints to keep her safe. We still haven't found that baby.

Hours later, I stretched a clean sheet over a recliner on the male side when "CODE GREEN Unit 3" blared over the intercom. I perked up like a dog at the sound of a squirrel,  and began glancing back and forth between the double doors and Kavon.

"Yeah, you can go." he chuckled, shaking his head.
Grinning, I bounded out the doors, through the courtyard, and cautiously stepped into unit 3. As I entered, I almost bumped into Allen, who was on his way out.

"It's over already?"
He looked disappointed. "Pretty much. It wasn't even a real code. I don't know why they called it."

My curiosity barked like a dog does at any noise from the door. Then I noticed Ray meandering out of room 6 and I beelined over there.

"Hey Ray, what's going on?"
Ray rolled his eyes and shook his head. "Poke your head in there and see for yourself."

I stepped in to see Dr. Kumar standing over a pale, gangly,

scraggly young man in blue paper scrubs who convulsed on the floor between the beds. Dr. Kumar's tired eyes narrowed in irritation.

"Roy, do you want Ativan?"

Roy stopped convulsing and looked up wide-eyed at Dr. Kumar.

"Yes," he muttered in surprise. No one had asked him that before. Instead, they always told him he wasn't getting Ativan. He wasn't sure how someone actually having a seizure would respond. He just knew he wanted Ativan. It's an addictive, sedating medicine that can be used to stop anxiety or, at higher doses, stop seizures.

"Alright, well we can't do that if you're laying there on the floor."

Confused, James sat up. Dr. Kumar turned to walk out and I followed, leaving James to scratch his head.

Dr. Kumar turned to me. "You're my witness, I never said that I'd give him Ativan. We've got thirty minutes left of this shift. It's really tempting just to order a saline injection and let the next Doctor deal with him."

# CHAPTER 8: **HIT ON**

Since  I don't want to bore you with the mundane details of the morning, let's fast forward to the following late afternoon. I moseyed through the courtyard back to PER after taking a patient to Unit Two. Looking up at the dusky blue sky, I took one last breath of fresh air before—*Bzzt*—entering the first set of PER doors. *It's almost sunset. At least I got to go outside again before dark*, I told myself as I waited for the double doors to shut behind me. With the onset of dusk came an onslaught of patients. Crunch time.  Before I had left,  every seat had been filled, even the few chairs where patients can sit while they wait to get checked in.

As soon as I stepped onto the patient floor, Jordan waved me over.

"Can you help me check these ladies in? We're swamped and I need to start skin checks." She nodded toward the growing line of women along the wall opposite me.

They all waited patiently—more or less—for their turn to get checked in. Some sat on the floor, staring off vacantly into space. Others stood with apprehensive eyes flicking back and forth across the room. Jordan's eyes looked worn down. We had shift change in a couple hours and she still hadn't gotten her break. Since she was a she, she was the only PER tech on our shift that could do female skin checks. Even though she got stuck with more work than the rest of us, that didn't mean she got more breaks.

"Do you want to take a break first?" I offered.

"Jordan, Jackie's ready to do the skin checks. I'm a take this one out to Four." Kavon shouted from the other side.

"I need to take my break," Jordan shouted back.

"It'll be real fast." He disappeared outside. Kavon put a lot of pressure on Jordan whenever we got a bunch of skin checks to do. As our team lead, he was under a lot of pressure to get patients in and out. The sooner they got their skin checks, the sooner we didn't have to wonder if they snuck in any razor blades.

Jordan grimaced. "Thanks anyways, Jay." She followed Jackie and a new patient to the bathroom.

I was the lone tech on this side now. If I got tunnel vision on one task, who knew what could erupt. I beckoned for one well-fed young woman to come up to get her picture taken and property packed. "Hi, I'm Jay, here to help you get checked in. First, let's get your picture for your chart."

"Ok."

"You got any questions while I set this up?"

When they're getting checked in, most people ask questions like, "When can I get something to eat?" "When will I get out of here?" or "Can I get a seat as far away as possible from that crazy person?" This patient had to be famished like the previous four new arrivals who had finished off the snack supply under the desk.

Instead of asking for food, she spurted out, "Do you think I'm sexy?"

I stopped my frantic typing, trying to hide my surprise as I looked back up at her over cups of untested urine samples sitting on the desk. *How did that question get into her head?* I asked myself. *Why didn't she ask about food or phones or safety like everybody else?* Just as my mouth formed the words "Not at all!" I realized how hurtful they could be. So I stuck with, "That's not appropriate" and immediately began typing more furiously than ever before.

She thought about it for a second and concluded, "Because this isn't a good place to meet someone?"

"Right," I replied, wondering how to get to the male side of the unit as soon as possible. Jordan had already rushed out the far doors for her overdue break, so this lady wasn't going anywhere anytime soon. Just two of us techs now, one for each side. Feeling stuck, I tried to get Kavon's attention so we could switch sides.

As the line of waiting women clamored for food, I picked up the snack crate and flipped it upside down on top of the desk.

"I'm sorry, I'm clean out. We'll get you some as soon as Jordan gets back."

I got a tirade from them.

"Hey Kavon, we're outta snacks. You got some down there?"

"Nah, I'm out too. Let me fix that." Destiny stood at the male side to cover him as he ran to the breakroom to restock.

"Iris? Your turn."

A woman built like a track star stood and strode over, her ponytail of black braids waving behind her.

"So, I'm Jay, I'll be taking care of you today. Can I have you take a seat at the side of the desk there so I can check your vital signs?"

"Sure." She replied stoically. She silently sat down in the weighted chair beside the desk. "Let's wait to talk until after we get your blood pressure, that way it's more accurate."

"Okay."

*So mild-mannered. She won't be here long,* I told myself. The machine began to hum when the break room door swung open and Kavon stepped out with a big grin and a basket of snacks. He set it down and slapped me on the shoulder.

"Hey there little man, you hear what went down at three last night?"

I glanced at him and smiled. His energy was contagious.

"I heard something but you always got the details, Kavon. Thanks for—" Iris cut in before I could finish.

"You're Kavon? You? You punk!" She leaped to her feet. I looked back to see Kavon's eyes bug out.

"Hey, hey let's keep it cool and calm. Cool and calm. Let's talk this out," he repeated.

"If you keep talking, I'll slap the-" she lunged forward,

swinging an open palm with the arm attached to the blood pressure cart. It jerked and teetered but didn't fall. Kavon bobbed out of reach. This was the time to shine with my MAM skills.

"Iris, Iris, you look furious. What's goin' on? You were just so calm."

She didn't even look at me. "You stay out of this. He needs to learn a lesson."

Kavon stared her back in the eye. I managed to stand between the two of them.

"Look, ma'am, I'm sorry about whatever it is you're angry about," he whispered.

"Don't you 'Look ma'am' me!" She ripped off the blood pressure cuff and jumped to the front of the desk. Kavon jumped for the door. Reaching over the desk, she grabbed the swivel chair from behind it and hurled it at him. He ducked back into the breakroom hall and the chair bounced off the door then clattered to the floor. As he closed the door, she leaped over the desk, fist raised. I heard a click just before she grabbed the handle. She turned it and pulled. It wouldn't budge. She jerked it a few more times then pounded on the window. "I'm coming for ya, #%&@*. You wait and see."

My jaw hung open. I stood there in shock, clutching the blood pressure cuff as she turned towards me. She transformed back into the original stoic Iris and sat down in the patient chair by the desk.

"He's gonna get it one of these days." Turning towards me, she asked, "Why don't you get me checked in so I can get my own spot?"

"Uh, well, uh, yes, Ma'am, I mean, yes Iris, or what do you like to be called?" I cautiously placed the cuff back on her arm.

"Iris is fine."

"Your pressure might come out a little high though after that."

"That's okay." I was dying to know what had happened between them, but if I asked her for details, she might make me die. The humming machine broke the awkward silence. I saw Kavon sneak back in on the male side with a basket of snacks. He quietly sat down at the desk where the rows of patients blocked him from view.

Later, Jordan came back from break on the wrong side, the male side. I still needed to switch before that first lady could make any more advances.

"Did I miss anything?" Jordan asked Kavon on the male side while she took the vest from him.

Kavon shot a glance at me as he shook his head.

"Nah, you didn't miss nothin'."

Jordan began rounding on the male side while Kavon and I continued to work feverishly, checking in the steady flow of newcomers. I heard someone attempting to sing and a chorus of laughter on the other side. No angry sounds, so I hardly even looked up as I zip-tied another patient's property. No time now. I could ask later. Jordan walked past the rows of recliners towards me as she scribbled in the binder.

"Let me know when you got several ready and I'll get a nurse so we can do their skin checks," she mumbled.

"There's already three ready. Here's the pictures of the new ones for your binder."

"Okay, let me get a nurse."

"Hey, Kavon!" I shouted. "Can we switch?" I didn't mention the Fisher of Compliments. Kavon sauntered over, laughing to himself.

"I bet Jordan would trade you. You missed it, this guy came over and started singing "You Are My Sunshine" at the top of his lungs to her," Kavon chortled. "She was so moved that she cried —and he was a terrible singer!" He let out another guffaw as I grinned at the thought.

Jordan let out a "Hmph."

I glanced over at Jordan and waited for a denial that never came. She gained a sudden fascination with the drawer of toothbrushes. *At least he didn't ask her if she thought he was sexy,* I told myself

"Kavon, was that lady that threw the chair an ex or what?"

"I don't know, but it's time I go on my break." Much later, Kavon finally took his lunch break. He always made sure the rest of the team got their lunch breaks before him.

We had been so busy he didn't have time to go until late. Waiting for things to calm down was always a gamble since more and more patients would arrive as the day went on.

A scraggly, pale guy holding a couple of towels from the linen cart trudged over.

"Hey Jay, can you unlock the bathroom so I can take a shower?"

"Yes—" I noticed a blue wristband indicating he needed someone at the door to make sure he didn't hurt himself. "Hold on, Can you wait ten minutes, Drake? Kavon will be back from break any minute now."

"I just need you to unlock the door. It doesn't take two guys to do that. Besides—" he nodded at a frail, elderly patient who wore a fall risk band on his wrist. "I don't need help showering."

"Sorry, Drake. We gotta have someone with their foot in the door while you're in there, so we gotta wait until we have enough staff."

"That's ridiculous! You let him—" he jutted a finger at 4B, whose eyes widened when he saw Drake pointing at him "—take one without anyone at the door and he took like twenty minutes."

"It's not the rule for everybody, Drake. Just people with a blue wristband like you got there. It's so we can make sure they don't hurt themselves."

Drake snorted. "Ah, come on, that's ridiculous. I'm not gonna try an' hurt myself in the shower"

"Sorry, it's the policy."

His tone turned hostile "That's bullshit! I'm not showering in front of nobody."

I glanced at the clock. 4:44. Come on, Kavon. All the quiet rooms were taken, so this could get real ugly real fast.

"We don't look, we face outside when we do it."

He rolled his eyes and sarcasm dripped from his voice. "Oh, okay. Everybody else here can see my bare ass but as long as it's not the guy at the door it's okay." His tone turned hostile again. "That's still bullshit! You already said yes and you're going back on your word." He threw his towels on the floor. I glanced at his hands again to make sure they weren't balled into fists.

"Sorry Drake, your safety is important to us."

He leered at me. "You know what, go #%&@ yourself, Jay." He turned to go back to his seat.

"That's physically impossible," I replied. *Dang it!* It slipped out before I realized it.

Drake swung around to face me. I heard a roar of laughter behind me and saw Kavon behind me with the dinner cart. Drake realized he'd risk losing a hot meal if he got out of hand and trudged back to his seat grumbling to himself.

Never before in my life had I made a decent comeback on the spot, and never again since then. I'm still quite proud of myself. So, I'd appreciate it if you'd highlight that story and tell your friends about it. I'm assuming you have friends, dear reader.

An hour later, Destiny popped out of the nurse station. "Looks like y'all need more work," she stated in her slight Southern accent. All the guys in row A who weren't asleep pivoted to face her like a flock of pigeons. She handed me a packet of papers matter-of-factly.

"Cora is ready to go, her dad is going to pick her up out front. Good luck." She disappeared as quickly as she had appeared. The men of row A stared forlornly at the door as it closed behind her. I found Cora's assigned seat. The figure of a small human lay draped by a big blanket, laying in the chair. That could be anyone. Whoever it is, she's probably sleeping.

I tried my usual soft approach. "Hey Cora, it's me, Jay."

What I presumed was the figure's head perked up at the sound of the name.

"Your ride is here."

The head immediately thudded back down on the chair and exuded a suspicious snore.

"Hey Cora, it'll be a lot easier to sleep at home." No movement.

I gently tapped the armrest, "Cora, are you okay?"

Still no movement. I tapped the headrest harder.

"Mmfff. Okay," came a bitter reply. She sat up and pulled the blanket off her head, revealing her short black hair and blue paper scrubs.

"Alright, I got your box and—" Cora's eyes abruptly squeezed shut and she fell back into the chair.

"Cooooraaaa."

"I'm coming," she groaned. She slowly scooted off the chair and rose to her feet. It didn't make her any taller because she was so short. Cora was the same age as me, but she moved like she was one hundred and three.

Once we got to the tech desk, I cut the zip ties on her box and pulled out a purse, jeans and a hoodie. "If you'll just sign here, we'll be good to go."

She plopped her head on the desk.

"Cora!" I hadn't heard any horror stories about her and wondered why they would have given such strong medication to this petite little lady. *Why would they discharge her like this?* I wondered. *Oh well, I'm not a doctor.* "Do you want to go change into your street clothes first?" I offered.

Jackie bustled by. "What's taking so long? Her dad has been calling from the front, Jay. Plus, we have six people in the waiting room."

Cora lowered her head.

"She's half asleep," I answered.

Undeterred, Destiny shook her shoulder. "Come on Cora, time to go. The doctor already decided and your dad has been waiting up front." I cut off her ID band and filed it away.

As Jackie looked on, we stood and—*Bzzzt*—I opened the first door for her. And then—*Bzzzt*—the second. We entered the sunlight, and I took a deep breath of fresh air. "Feels good to get out, huh?"

Her eyes scrunched as if she had woken at 3:00 AM. I began walking but realized I was leaving her behind. She barely trudged along. Any slower and she would fall right over. I turned back around and matched her shuffling pace. It felt like I was going backward in time.

Deandre passed us on the sidewalk and did a double-take. "She's getting discharged?"

"Yeah," I muttered.

"She looks like she's about to fall over, you sure you got the right person?"

I averted my gaze."Yeah, I checked her wristband."

We began to pass the cafeteria as Chantelle walked out. She stared at Cora, who continued to trudge as if this was a death march. Chantelle turned her gaze to me as she raised an eyebrow. She didn't need to say anything.

"Destiny told-" I started explaining before withering under her stare. "Cora, let's go back and double-check."

We turned back to PER and Cora picked up the pace, which meant now she was going as fast as I could crawl.

I burst into the nurse station and strode up to Destiny who turned a quizzical eye.

"Jay, Cora's dad has called three more times. Did you see him at the front?"

"We just made it halfway to the front but she can hardly walk. If she were any more sedated I'd have to drag her. Why is she getting discharged?"

A squeak came from behind me and I turned. The squeak came from Dr. Miller's chair as he pivoted to face me. It sounded like a cry of distress under the weight of his massive frame.

"I already saw her. She's malingering. She's okay, she just doesn't want to go," he told me.

"How many chairs do you go through in a week, Doctor?" I began the question and caught myself. "How-kay. I'll take her. But she doesn't have maybe a broken leg or something?"

"No. It's all an act."

I didn't think Cora could walk any slower, but she proved me wrong when we walked back out. She would be frozen in space if I wasn't carrying her purse for her. As we passed the cafeteria, Jack led a group of patients out. They all stared at the two of us. I hung my head, wishing I could bury it in the sand. *This looks like malpractice. Dr. Miller should be doing this himself!* I silently lamented.

Jack's mouth hung open. "She's getting discharged?"

"Yeah, and this is her purse, not mine. Ask me about it later." *Bzzzt*—I buzzed us into the front, and she trudged inside. Immediately, I scanned the room for a middle-aged male.

"Cora! We missed you so much!" A small, gentle-looking man rushed over to us, his arms outstretched. He beamed beneath his glasses and baseball cap. Rushing along beside him came a skinny girl whose grin sparkled with braces.

Cora perked up and her demeanor transformed in an instant, as if we had just given her an IV of espresso. "Hey, Dad! Hey, Sis! I missed you too!" They wrapped each other in a warm group embrace and didn't let go. They seemed to radiate as they cherished each other. I felt that I stood on hallowed ground.

"I can't believe you came all this way, Dad! I didn't wanna come 'cause they told me my dad was picking me up and I thought it was step-dad."

Her father embraced her tighter "Don't worry about him, honey. We're going home. I'd come from Antarctica to get you if I had to."

As they released their embrace, I sheepishly handed Cora her discharge packet. "Oh yeah," she piped up, pointing to me. "This is my boyfriend."

I froze as my face flushed. I hadn't seen that coming. My mind raced. *That rumor could get me fired. I've known her for twenty minutes and I just opened the door for her and carried her purse. That's it!*

They all laughed and I began breathing again. I glanced sideways at the secretary to see if she had overheard. She didn't look up from her newspaper. *I'm not opening the door for anybody anymore,* I swore to myself.

Some people end up here because they pose a danger to others and I'm happy they made it in. Some people end up here because they pose a danger to themselves and I'm happy they made it in too. Some people end up here because someone else posed a danger to them and I'm happy they left the situation, but appalled to know that whoever harmed them still runs around freely.

Later that day, Marva from triage escorted a wizened woman in her 60's over to the chair by the desk. The woman's right eye was swollen with big splotches of brown, purple, and blue. Her forearms and shoulder did too. Anger boiled inside me. *What monster would beat an old lady?* I asked myself.

"Hi, I'm Jay, I'll be helping take care of you this shift." I fought the urge to ask directly what low-life harmed her and where they lived.

"Hola, I am Estela. I can take care of myself."

Taken aback, I pivoted like a politician. "So what brings you here today, Estela?"

"My family doesn't like that I keep going for walks because they think that I will get lost." She shook her head. "They locked me inside the house and went to get groceries, but I wanted to go for a walk. So I jumped out the window and found they also had locked the gate. So I jumped over the fence too. I fell when I landed and some pendejo called the police."

Not what I expected. I felt somewhat relieved that no one else had caused her bruises. "That's impressive, you don't let anything stop you," I told her. I really meant, "Thanks for the heads up. We'll keep a close eye on you."

Fortunately, she did not escape, at least not during my shift. As I drove home, I wondered how distressed her family must feel trying to safely respect her freedom.

The next day started like any other. In our haste to get everything done before chaos erupted, we hit the late morning lull earlier than usual. I paced up and down the male side to keep myself from nodding off. *I'm so bored, I'm ready to gouge my eyes out just to give myself something to do,* I complained to myself. *On second thought, I'd better not say that out loud or they might put me in a quiet room.* I had already swept twice, cleaned the bathroom, stocked the drawers, and sanitized the patient phones. For the fourth time that morning, I asked Kavon what I could do to help.

"Why don't you take your break?" He chuckled, "You look like a caged lion."

The door to the break room hallway opens up right next to the tech desk on the female side. After my break, I stepped back into PER on the female side and paused as my eyes adjusted to the dim light. In my peripheral vision, I noticed blue behind the desk, instead of the green the techs wore. If we got really busy, sometimes the nurses would cover for us so we could go eat, but it wasn't really busy and it was not the royal blue the nurses wear. It was the sky blue of the paper scrubs patients can wear. I slowly approached the desk. A young woman with long black hair and olive-toned skin sat serenely in the high-back swivel chair behind the desk with her feet under her. She looked like a queen observing her subjects. While I wondered how she got there without anyone noticing, I heard the pitter-patter of feet approaching quickly from the male side.

"Get some pants!" Jordan shouted.

I grimaced and looked up at the ceiling. *Never, never ever assume people are wearing pants,* I reminded myself. That's rule number thirty-seven of PER: Never assume patients are wearing pants. I didn't want to appear like an aggressor, so I sprinted to the laundry cart, grabbed a poncho, and approached the desk backward as best as I could without tripping. Jordan grabbed it and wrapped the young lady up, evicting her from her throne.

Later, Jordan and I updated drug test results over a couple of containers of urine.

"Do you wanna take a seat, Jordan?"

"Are you serious? Do you know what's been in that seat, Jay?"

I glanced down at the black chair. "I didn't think of that." No one from our team would sit in that chair for days.

Suddenly, screams from the waiting room began punctuating our sentences.

"We'd better get a room ready," Jordan interjected.

"What am I missing here?" I asked as I stood up. I trusted her instinct, but there was nothing unusual about noisy individuals in the waiting room. I would be noisy too if I were stuck in handcuffs.

"Did you see the two guys fighting, and the police had to pull them apart?" she replied, staring at the video footage through the triage window. I pictured two handcuffed fellows fighting like chickens, headbutting and ramming each other while trying not to lose their balance. If I were the one letting them in, I'd be tempted to procrastinate just to see who would win. At the rate they were going, they would probably break through the wall first.

Jackie called me over. "We need to make room for those new guys." She handed me a stack of patient files. "So round up these people and take them to PER 2."

"You got it."

"Thanks, sweetie."

"I'm telling HR you called me that."

"Go ahead. They're just gonna call you sweetie, too."

Ten minutes later, a line of patients shuffled along behind me on our way to the "good behavior" overflow unit. You could always tell who needed to go to the overflow unit by the horrified look on their face as they sat upright in their recliner in PER, unable to sleep as they took in all the chaos they had stumbled into. The people in PER who acted as comfortable as if they were in their own living room were the ones to keep an eye on. There was a reason they weren't shocked or scared. They fit in too well.

Those who could, carried their zip-tied boxes of belongings. I pushed the rest of the boxes on a dolly. We passed through the double doors of the emergency unit while Chris guarded the exit to make sure no one tried to slip out with them. When they stepped out of the dusky unit into the sunlight, I could see their faces more clearly. The door shut, muffling the shocking sounds of chaos behind us. A young Cuban woman breathed a sigh of relief. She had never been in a place like this before. In contrast, a short, bronze middle-aged woman's weathered face appeared almost bored. She had been here too many times to count. A tall, lanky man with a grizzled face grinned as he savored the fresh air. He had been in there for two days, in the dark, where day blended into night, without access to the outdoors. If someone wasn't delirious when they came in, they very well could be when they came out.

As we walked through the courtyard, I chatted with them about what they missed from outside the hospital. The smörgåsbord of human experiences shared common threads: a yearning to hug one's child, the joy of a dog dancing in excitement to see you, and of course, the freedom to pick what one ate.

After we entered the overflow unit, the weathered woman asked me where I was from.

"Here, well not this facility, but this state," I replied, keeping it as vague as possible.

"You're lucky to be home. I have to take the Greyhound to the other side of the country to get back to my son."

I turned to leave.

"Before you go, there's something I want to tell you."

I turned back and looked around. We stood in the middle of twenty patients, which led me to believe there wasn't a risk of anything inappropriate.

"Okay, I'm listening."

"I go by chief executive officer because no one believes me whenever I say that I'm the president. Let's go to dinner. I could make you rich and hire you to be in my secret service."

I might have taken her up on it if I hadn't just received a five-cent raise.

As dusk turned dark and we reached the last hour of our shift, the police brought in Aba. As soon as the exuberant, middle-aged woman came in from triage, she declared in a booming Nigerian accent, "Let's get this party started," and anything else that popped into her mind. Quite a few things popped into her mind.

"Come sit down so I can get your blood pressure," Chris told her.

"I'm cold, give me a hug," she responded.

Chris decided to go on break.

Since it was my turn with the vest, I rounded across the periphery of the unit noting where everyone was. Aba's voice reached every corner. I found her hilarious. This late in the shift, I was drained to exhaustion and welcomed the comic relief.

Aba looked so comfortable, so cheery, as if she was at a sleepover at her best friend's house rather than crammed in a room full of strangers who weren't sent here based on good behavior.

Chris returned in a sour mood. Usually calm and philosophical, he stood by the desk on the female side with his eyes narrowed and brow furrowed in irritation as he checked the results on the cups of urine arrayed across the desk.

"You look like you just took a shot of one of those cups. What happened, Chris?" I asked.

"Aba's here." He sullenly scowled as if her very name had a bitter taste.

Meanwhile, she sat in a recliner wrapped in a blanket and smiling as brightly as if it was her birthday party. I then realized that she was a frequent flier, even though this was my first time meeting her. The rest of the team had seen her too many times for their liking.

"Thirty minutes left of this shift. At least she didn't come in sooner," Chris tried to console himself.

As if she heard her name, Aba turned towards him, gazing at Chris's stocky frame garnished with curly hair, and asked in her booming voice, "Is it possible for you to sleep with me?"

Chris's eyes narrowed as he let out a groan. "Technically, yes," he muttered. He set down the cup of urine and backed even farther away. "Just twenty-nine minutes left of this shift."

Seated at the desk, Jorge pulled out a granola bar and began to munch surreptitiously.

It wasn't surreptitious enough to escape Aba's ears.

"What are you doing? You don't need that, you're fat! I will save you, give me your food." Blushing, Jorge said something about using the bathroom and stepped out the back door.

Everyone that comes in deserves something to eat. I brought her a ham and cheese sandwich in plastic wrap.

She looked up at me and smiled mischievously. "Will you marry me?"

"Be quiet," Chris demanded in exasperation from the other side of the room.

"No my voice is sexy, everyone wants to hear it," she shouted back. My abs hurt from laughing.

"Just seventeen minutes left," Chris kept muttering to himself.

I hesitantly turned to him. "You know that clock's broken, right?"

We almost had to call a Code Green on him.


A few shifts later, a man with a head of curly black hair waited ever so patiently to get checked in. He didn't fit in. Most people started complaining loud enough for the whole unit to hear if they weren't sitting in a recliner within ten minutes. Besides his calm behavior, his appearance stood out with his clean shirt, fitted jeans, and polished shoes. He had sat there serenely, back to the wall, observing the unit for the last thirty minutes. I felt bad for him. The obnoxious ones got all the attention.

"Okay brother, it's finally your turn." He walked over and

plopped down in the hot seat  and pulled out his phone, ready to drop it in the bin as nonchalantly as if he were depositing a check. *Finally, someone who's compliant and smells nice,* I thought to myself.

"Can you verify your name and date of birth?"

"Robby, XX/XX/XXXX," he obliged, staring straight past me.

"Robby? Weren't you here last week?"

"Yeah."

"Oh man, you doing okay?"

"Yeah," he replied, still staring straight ahead.

I paused in disbelief. "No really, what brings you here today? People don't just come back here to visit."

"Same old."

Hopefully, he would be more open with the Doctor, or he would never leave this place.

"Well you know the drill, we're just waiting for the skin exam and then Kenisha, the one in that fluorescent vest, will set you up with one of those chairs."

"I know."

Eons later, when all the usual chaos inside the nursing station simmered down, Kurt, the heaviest nurse on the unit, came out to do skin checks.

"Finally, we've got five guys waiting," I remarked. "Robby, you're up."

"It's okay, he can go first." Robby nodded at the elderly man next to him.

*What a considerate guy,* I marveled. Robby let the next three men go ahead as well.

After the third one, Kurt paused. "Jackie's waving at me from the nurse station, I think I got a call from unit 3. I'll come back whenever it's done." He walked away, opened the nursing station door, and entered another realm of chaos.

"Sorry, Robby."

"It's okay."

I started tapping on the nurse station windows to see

which nurse could come and finish these skin checks.

"I got you." Jackie stepped out onto the patient floor and marched over with her clipboard.

"Let's get this over with, who's next?"

Robby stood up with a glimmer of a half smile. Most men did when she came by. Without stopping, she marched on past the rows of recliners and into one of the patient bathrooms. I followed Robby in.

"Okay, we need to check for any wounds or weapons. Let's make this quick, leave your boxers on, everything else comes off," Jackie declared in a monotone voice.

If you didn't do this a dozen times a day, it would sound very unprofessional. Robby stood there in his boxers, expressionless while Jackie marked her clipboard. Her brow furrowed and her eyes darted up from her notes. "Weren't you here last week?"

"Yeah."

"What brings you here today?"

His eyes widened and he stared her in the eye. "To see you."

I stifled a laugh and waited for him to propose with a toilet paper ring, possibly the same one that Destiny declined earlier.

Jackie didn't flinch. Her eyes narrowed. "Turn around." She glanced at his back and checked off her last box. "Okay, we're done." She whipped open the door, stepped out, and slammed it shut. No toilet paper ring. What a disappointment. Maybe he had an emergency and had to use it.

As Robby nonchalantly put his shirt back on, I gave the usual spiel about the urine drug test. I hate to admit it, but I couldn't wait to see what he would say next. At the same time, I couldn't help but fear for his fate. The charge nurse is the last person you want mad at you. As tempting as it was to heckle her about it, I didn't dare to.

# CHAPTER 9: **TAPPED OUT**

Sunday: the quietest day of the week. Quiet because all the boisterous people who got high out of their minds and drunk as a skunk had already arrived on Friday night and went in-patient to detox on Saturday. Despite the quiet, the new arrivals still weren't any happier about getting stuck here. Checking in grouchy man after grouchy man got old fast. I don't blame them, I'd be grouchy too if I was stuck with an empty stomach in a dim room full of strangers who had broken enough social norms to get here. I paused as an epiphany struck. *Hold on now, I'm stuck with an empty stomach in a dim room full of strangers who had broken enough social norms to get here.* I then realized that I felt just as grumpy as they did. "Okay, NEXT," I shouted.

A scrawny young man strode over. His unruly black hair made him look less short than he actually was. As he sat down in the chair next to the desk, I wondered why he wasn't scowling like all the other guys.

"Hi, I'm Jay. You been here before?"

We touched knuckles.

"Nah, man this place is a trip. I'm Juan by the way. How's your day been?"

"Alright." I slapped the blood pressure cuff onto his arm, pressed START, and waited for a reading while it hummed merrily.

"So, what brings you here today?"

"Ah man, I made a joke about death at the grocery store and next thing I know the cops brought me here."

Fighting the urge to ask what the joke was, I rattled off Peaceful Pines policies as I took his picture, plunked his shoes into a bin, and wrapped up the paperwork.

Kavon and Kurt stepped out of a patient bathroom. They were just doing skin checks.

"Alright Jay, we got anybody else?"

"Yeah. Okay, Juan, that's Kavon over there. They're gonna take care of that skin check I told you about."

Juan turned to go. "Okay, thanks, Jay."

"You're wel-" I stopped in surprise. *Hold on a second, did he just say thanks?* I wondered. *That was a nice guy. I hope he gets out soon.* I hadn't heard 'thanks' in so long that it felt like a foreign language. "So long" meaning the last few hours.

Kavon came down the aisle.

"I gotta go talk with Jackie about a situation and Kurt is itching to get back to the nurse station. Chris, you go do this skin."

Chris scowled. "I just talked to you this morning about how disrespectful it is to order us around instead of *asking*. I'm not your servant."

Kavon stopped and looked Chris in the eye.

"You got your panties in a knot," he told Chris before walking away.

Chris glowered, then turned to Juan."Okay Juan come with me."

Later on that morning, a husky man stood in the middle of the back row and raised his ebony-toned arms. My muscles tightened, ready to leap over there before he did something to his slumbering neighbors.

"It's the LORD'S DAY AND I'M GONNA PRAISE HIM. HALLELUJAH, I SEE THE LIGHT," he shouted. He sat back down without another sound.

"Happy Sunday, sir?" I replied in confusion.

"That's DJ," Chris muttered from beside me as he dug into his yogurt cup. He didn't care for management's rules like no staff eating on the patient side. "Don't be fooled by that holy man act. Last time they admitted him to an in-patient unit he seduced a female patient into the bathroom with him."

Kavon turned from cleaning a recliner. "He actually did

that twice at different units. That man got game."

"Hey!" Jackie poked her head out of the nurse station. "We got a patient in triage that only speaks ASL and they sent us an interpreter. Will one of you go up front and bring her? "

The three of us froze and exchanged glances. I sure didn't want to go because I didn't want to miss whatever DJ was going to blurt out next. Chris slowly lowered his yogurt out of her line of sight. He didn't care for the rules, but he hated lectures.

She stepped out. "Did somebody sedate you guys? Chris— you stop eating that in front of the patients and go, and on the way back bring me back one of those yogurts from the cafeteria." Chris scowled as he turned to leave. "I'm not your waiter," he muttered under his breath.

Jackie had already turned back towards the nurse station. Without turning around she shouted. "Blueberry. And don't forget a spoon!"

A bit later Chris came back from the front, smoothing his curly man bun as he—*Bzzzt*— opened the unit door and held it open for a slender, red-headed young woman. I'd never seen a spring in his step before. All of a sudden he loved his job.

"Aw, thank you, Chris," she told him.

Like a flock of seagulls, the heads of half the sleepy back row snapped up and swiveled toward her harmonious voice. Chris grinned and power walked past her to the nurse station. "Let me get the nurse station door for—*Bzzzt*—you, Mandy. I'll introduce you to the charge nurse."

Kavon and I looked at each other and chuckled.

"He's like a new man," I observed.

"Yeah Jay, but he better pray DJ don't steal her away."

When my turn came to go to lunch, I handed off the fluorescent vest to Chris. "She won't be able to take her eyes off you when you wear this," I told him.

"What are you talking about?" he asked.

"Oh, you know what I'm talking about."

He put it on and zipped it up. He never zips it up. Then

he randomly decided to go monitor the other side of the room where Mandy stood in the middle of the back row, signing between a patient and Destiny.

He turned back to me. "It looks kinda baggy, doesn't it? Isn't there a medium size one buried in that desk?"

"Probably, but I'm on lunch." I high-tailed it before he could ask me to dig it out.

In the cafeteria, I carried a  tray of steaming ribs and mashed potatoes, forcing myself not to chow down until I was seated. With all the walking we did, I felt ravenous. I dug in, splattering BBQ sauce on my hands and front. I was too hungry to care. As I dug in for another bite, the intercom crackled overhead, "CODE GREEN P-E-R! CODE GREEN, P-E-R!"

I'd never heard it sound so desperate. I looked down forlornly at my plate in denial. *There weren't any really big patients in PER today. I'm sure Chris and Kavon got it under control,* I tried to convince myself.

SCR-EEEE-EEE—Deandre's metal chair slid across the floor as he jumped up and hustled  out, leaving his tray behind.

What was I thinking? *Those were my brothers*, I told myselfI made a quick bargain with my stomach by shoveling down another bite before rushing out behind Deandre. Hopefully, I wouldn't choke on the way over.

On entering PER, I followed a flood of green and blue swarming the middle of the back row. I stood on tiptoe, trying to peek over the sea of staff. Even if I had on a pair of stilts, I still couldn't see because my eyes hadn't adjusted to the dark yet. Whoever it was had to be big and ruthless for that many nurses to come out of the station like that. Once my eyes adjusted, I saw glimpses of Mandy's terrified face, her hands tugging on an arm wrapped around her neck from behind. What little color there was had drained from her face.  Whoever had her in a choke hold was too short for me to spot. Kavon and Chris pried at the attacker's arms as Mandy gasped for air like a fish out of water.

As I dashed down to the female side, they peeled the

assailant's arm off and pinned him against the wall. I couldn't believe my eyes as they dragged him to the quiet room where Destiny stood, buckling the restraints across the bed. *Juan?* When I met Juan, I never imagined he'd give us any trouble, much less end up in restraints. *Hopefully, he didn't inspire any of the other patients.* Whenever anyone gets put in restraints we're required to have a staff member at arms distance at all times. Now we would be down a team member.

Chris came out of the quiet room, smoothing his unruly hair. "Kavon is doin' the one-to-one." He scanned the room. "Where'd Mandy go?"

Destiny smirked. "As soon as you broke that chokehold, she booked it outta here."

Chris's face went crestfallen.

"What a welcome to PER. She's probably halfway across the state by now," Destiny continued.

Chris glared at her. "It's not funny. Someone almost got choked out."

"You're just mad you didn't get her number," she replied.

Chris glared at her as he scratched his goatee with his middle finger. Back to his old self. That didn't last long.

# CHAPTER 10: **ONE** ON **ONE**

Of all the roles we play— bargainer, confidant, protector, food source, etc.—my least favorite role is doing the one-to-one. Whoever received that assignment had to stay within arm's length of the patient, who for some reason or another needed that extra precaution to protect themselves, or others, or both. Usually one-to-one's happened because a patient was in restraints or had a penchant for walking that exceeded their ability to stay upright.

I arrived early for night shift as the sun sank below the horizon. The array of pastel rays highlighted the clouds in a colorful goodbye. I felt a twinge of guilt as I thought of those patients cooped up in the emergency unit whose only view of the sky came through a 6-inch strip of reinforced glass.

Sporting a half smile, I arrived as excited for the night shift as one could be. Then Trey, the PER shift team lead, looked me in the eye. "You're at Unit 3 for a one-to-one tonight."

"Oh." I turned around as that half smile twisted down into a half frown in childish distaste. When I entered Unit 3, it took me a minute to realize who I was taking over for. No frail figure trying to get up, no sulking shadow in the isolation room, plucking at restraints. Just a short slender young man nonchalantly playing checkers with Damion from day shift. The patient looked more like me than anyone else on the unit.

"Hello," boomed the young man in a jovial tone as I approached. "I'm Alex."

He seemed so good-natured and healthy that I wondered why he would need someone within arms reach. I should have taken a suggestion from the exhaustion emitted from Damion's drooping eyelids.

"Hey Jay. Good luck," Damion muttered before leaving to

clock out. I sat down in his place.

"He was losing, let's start over," Alex stated in a thick Argentine accent. In one swoop, he swept all the checkers off the board.

"Okay," I replied. I couldn't help but feel disappointed in Damion's checker skills. He had a degree in psychology and was already halfway through a Master's, but I guess it didn't translate over to the checkerboard.

Testing Alex's acumen, I slid a checker—the bait—forward one space and waited to see if he would bite. Given where we were, I need to specify *figuratively* bite. Without blinking, he grabbed his targeted piece and jumped it just as I planned, but then lifted it again even though there was no legal space for him to jump again. He launched it four spaces over and swept up three of my pieces as if he had completed a perfectly legitimate move.

"Gotcha! Hehe," he snickered.

In first grade we had some creative moves in checkers, like the "tornado" but whatever this was, it took the cake. I decided to try his tactic and leaped my piece over four spaces and collected his checkers just like he had done to me.

"No, no, that's not allowed," Alex bellowed as his eyes narrowed in disdain.

My eyes widened in surprise and I debated whether or not to continue this fool's errand. He reclaimed his pieces and commenced a blitzkrieg on the board. I sat there motionless, resigned to defeat until the board lay barren of my pieces.

Next, at his request, we played chess. I stifled my surprise as he quietly played by the rules. We respectfully took turns, taking a pawn here and a bishop there without any qualms. He then moved his queen into my trap. *Time to reclaim my dignity from that checkers game*, I thought. When I swooped up his queen, his jaw lowered in disbelief.

"This game is *stupid*!" he shouted, flipping the board over and spilling the pieces across the table.

I don't know why I was surprised by this after what I saw

in the checkers game, but I was. I kicked myself, *Should have played it easy on him.* I had to admit that flipping the board over was pretty effective for avoiding a loss. *What would have happened had I tried that in the organic chemistry exam that I flunked,* I wondered.

Alex eventually retreated to the "quiet" room, much to the relief of the entire unit, except for myself, since I was obliged to join him. He had gotten so out of control, they just assigned him there so they wouldn't have to keep moving him from a regular room. Alex sprawled out on the bed riveted to the floor and then immediately sat back up.

"I want to take a shower. You could use one too."

I pretended to wipe my forehead in order to get a whiff of my underarm. *Not bad for 8:00 pm.* The isolation room had no bathroom unless you count a handheld urinal brimming with something that wasn't water. I wanted to avoid looking at it, but I also wanted to avoid seeing it overflow or get thrown at me.

"Alright, Alex, let's grab you some towels and empty the urinal on the way over."

He kindly carried the urinal while I grabbed a stack of towels and toiletries. When we got to the bathroom, I laid a towel in front of the shower and turned the water on to warm up while he stood by the sink.

"I want to take a shower."

"Well, you can see if it's warm enough for you. Let me flush that urinal for you."

"It's okay," he replied. He raised the urinal up toward the ceiling. "I'm going to take a warm shower."

*He just wants to get a reaction out of me before he dumps it into the sink,* I told myself. Then I saw him tip it toward his head, and my mouth dropped in horror.

I reached up to try and stop it. "No, *don't*—"

"Oh baby!" he shouted as the contents cascaded over his head and splattered on the floor around us. Hearing my shout, Deandre burst into the bathroom

"What's goin' on?"

"He just dumped it on himself," I retorted in disbelief, pointing at the now empty urinal. The only way this could get worse is if he accused me of dumping it on him.

Deandre hardly raised an eyebrow. "Okay. Why am I not surprised?" He turned to Alex. "Now, go get in the shower Alex."

I wondered how Deandre planned to enforce that command without wrestling a man who was covered in, well, we'll just call it an unpleasant liquid.

To my surprise, Alex walked into the shower without making a move at us. He did shout some obscenities in his native language. I would have written down the new words if I wasn't busy washing my hands up to my elbows.

After Alex finished his shower, he came out just in time for group. Thankfully, he got dressed before coming out for group. Not everyone here remembered to do things in that order, and I had my suspicions about him.

Adults of every age, size, shape, and color sat around the semicircle of sofas and chairs, in varying degrees of interest or lack thereof.

Deandre, who sat in front of them, asked "What do you all want to talk about today?"

"Buddha," shouted Alex.

Deandre groaned. "Which one?"

"Me," Alex answered. He then turned to me. "You are the white Buddha, I am the brown Buddha."

*Finally, a patient that doesn't point out how skinny I am,* I told myself.

Deandre pivoted. "You know, Buddha talked about letting go of the pain of the past so that one might enjoy the present."

Janet caught on and piped up before Alex had time to speak. "My favorite quote from the Buddha is 'If you want to fly, give up everything that weighs you down.'"

As she finished her sentence, she turned toward Leslie, who had nodded off. Janet elbowed her in the ribs.

"Ow, you—" Leslie caught Janet's eye and glanced at Alex.

"—Oh, I really like what you said, Janet, whatever it was. What do you think, Frank?"

Frank caught the drift, "I think he said something like 'Better to remain silent and be thought a fool than to speak and to remove all doubt.'" He turned over to Alex and glared.

Dominic grinned, "I like that quote but that was Abraham Lincoln, brother."

Alex refused defeat. He stood up, raised his hands above his head, and skipped around the center of the group as he wriggled his hips, singing in his thick accent "I'm so sexy, sexy, sexy. I'm so sexy, sexy, sexy."

A cacophony of chiding voices around the room barraged him, demanding, pleading, begging him to stop. He only shook his hips harder and sang even louder, "I'M SO SEXY, SEXY, SEXY!"

"Alright, we get it, you're sexy," Deandre snapped.

"You know it," responded Alex. He then sat down quietly satisfied with the attention he got.

Angela let out a sigh of relief and chimed, "So you were saying something about focusing on the present, Deandre."

"Yes, thank you Ang—"

"I'M SO SEXY, SEXY, SEXY!"

After several valiant attempts at taking the reins from Alex in the group discussion, Deandre stood up.

"Well, everybody, it's getting late, let's call it a day and try again tomorrow. Thanks to each one of you for coming to group."

Angela jumped up

"Good night Deandre and Jay." She zipped straight over to her room.

Frank slowly rose from his chair, his old knees crackling. "Oh man, that sounds great. Thanks for trying, Deandre. Have a good night." He shuffled off.

Half the group had already beelined for their rooms. They couldn't stand Alex any longer. The rest either sat staring thoughtfully into space or scribbling madly in their journals. I kept tensed to restrain Alex in case he tried to give us any more surprises.

Dominic slapped his journal shut. "Well, that was a horrendous ending to group. I'm sorry. Good night Deandre."

"Good night, Dominic. Thanks for your comments"

Alex remained uncharacteristically quiet. He turned to face me and then back at the other patients who wished each other good night outside their rooms.

"Fools! They think it's night! Anyone can see it's clear as day."

I did a double take at the wide reinforced window that ran across the wall in front of us. Pitch black.

"What do you see out there Alex?" I tried.

"Don't question me, you fool. I've had enough of these fools." He marched to the isolation room and I cautiously followed him.

"Do you need to go to the bathroom?"

"No."

"At all?"

"No."

He sat down on the bed and I dragged a chair beside it, debating how close to sit next to him. Alex picked up a tabloid magazine from a stack in the corner and pointed to the woman on the cover.

"This is my girlfriend, Chelsea. I met her online. We send each other lots of messages and she loves me. Sometimes I send her money except when I'm mad. She stopped talking to me so I broke up with her."

Before I could question why he used the present tense "is," he tossed it aside and picked up the next magazine, pointing to a perfume ad he had bookmarked.

"This is Stephanie. She is my girlfriend too. We talk online all the time. We are going to get married sometime, I just have to tell her."

I nodded, amused but poker-faced. Deandre shuffled by in the vest, doing his rounds. He proffered a sympathetic glance. I smiled at him. I was just happy that Alex hadn't spilled any more bodily fluids.

Alex sat on his bed staring at the wall before opening up. "I came to this country with my mother to play professional tennis, but then they brought me here. I can't see my mom but she brings me these magazines so I don't get bored."

I thought of what his mother must be going through right now. Reflecting on a mother's love eased the frustration I felt about spending a shift with him. I felt a twinge of guilt at getting so irked at him. It was nothing compared to the overwhelming worry she must be going through.

"Speaking of bored, I want to go exercise," he declared.

"Alex, it's 9:30 pm."

"You're just jealous that I will get all the women because my muscles are bigger than yours."

I stifled a retort as he grabbed the doorknob.

"Alex, let's play a game."

"A game?"

"Yes, a game of endurance. Let's see who can stay in the room the longest, you or I."

"You know you are going to lose?"

"Prove it," I replied.

He sat back down. "Okay."

I prayed this wouldn't backfire. "But a couple rules first. It's okay to go to the bathroom as long as you don't miss and you come straight back. And you can't do something that would make the other person obliged to leave."

"Like what?"

"Anything." I wasn't about to give him any ideas.

"What does the winner get?"

I hadn't thought that far ahead. My mind raced, noting the graham cracker wrappers scattered across the floor. We have boxes upon boxes of them in the storage room. "Six packages of graham crackers," I stammered.

"Psh, I already have ten of those." he lifted up the mattress pad to reveal his stash.

"Bragging rights?"

"Oh, haha, you are on."

We shook hands. I fought the urge to scramble for hand sanitizer. That would derail our progress.

He picked up a Sharpie and began to draw mustaches on the celebrities in his magazines.

"Who gave you a Sharpie?" I asked, meaning *Who was crazy enough to let you have that?*

"You."

"What?"

"You."

I patted my scrub pocket and discovered that my Sharpie was missing. I decided to wait to reclaim it until after he fell asleep.

"How the—"

He pointed the uncapped Sharpie at me.

"What do you want a tattoo of? I am a great artist."

"No thanks."

"Don't be a pansy."

"Sorry Alex, I'm a pansy."

He began writing on the wall. I jumped over and wrestled the Sharpie out of his hands.

Rushing out, I tossed it behind the nurse station. My hands had streaks across them, but at least my face was unmarred. On second thought, I tossed my scissors over there as well. I wasn't taking any chances.

Alex poked his head out of the doorway, grinning wide as a jack-o-lantern."You lose!"

"Thud!" That was my palm hitting my forehead."Okay Alex, best out of 5, like tennis."

He eventually dozed off and I walked back and forth in the tiny room, expecting him to jump up as soon as I sat down. Eventually, my head began to nod as I stood in place. I did some air squats to wake up and then sat down. My eyelids began to grow heavy. I'll just close them for a minute, I told myself. My head bobbed up and down.

I felt a hand on my shoulder and my eyes snapped open, arms tensed, ready to fend off an attack.

"Jay, are you okay?"

I looked up into Darius's concerned eyes. "Yes." I stood to show that I wasn't groggy. I felt I had closed my eyes for a minute, but daylight now brightened the room. As Director of Tech's, he would surely write me up for this. I felt too tired to care.

His face emitted empathy. Darius had worked as a tech once too. He knew what night shifts were like. "Alex is really sick. He needs a lot of attention. I'll relieve you from the one-to-one until Ray gets here."

What a leader. That man deserves a raise.

After night shift, my coworkers Deandre, Ally, and Ruby sat together in the cafeteria and ate breakfast. Deandre, who had worked in psychiatry for almost a decade, told of a time when Chelsea, the bubbly, happy-go-lucky HR manager led a group of potential hires through the grounds, explaining what a great place this was for patients to recover at. All of a sudden, a patient exploded through the doors of a nearby unit and high-tailed it across the grass like a gazelle. Just as suddenly, a stocky tech burst out of the unit doors after him at a dead sprint. He tackled the man, then stood over him and shouted, "I got you!" with the bravado of a linebacker deluded by the Super Bowl. The tour members looked on in shock, as the poor manager attempted to sweep up the scraps of their burst bubble along with their jaws. That tech no longer works at Pleasant Pines.

Ruby piped up, "They shouldn't have fired him, he worked hard and we're always short staffed. We got to protect ourselves. We can't do that with those weak sauce de-escalation moves. You see me limping 'cause I tore my meniscus at a code a while back. You try to "manage aggression" with MAM and their fists are gonna manage your nose. You know what we need? We need BAM like they got at Metroplex Hospital's psych facility. My friend who worked there got trained in BAM—Behavioral Adjusting Maneuvers. Their catchphrase is "The employee will be unharmed and the threat *neutralized*." They shut it down because the troublemakers kept getting taken to the ER in a stretcher, but in six years my friend never got a scratch."

# CHAPTER 11: **SPIT IT OUT**

My mind raced as I walked from the parking lot to PER. *My first full night shift in PER. How am I going to stay alert all night?* I anxiously opened the break room door. To my surprise, all of the other techs were already there early. Nothing like day shift. Looking around, I knew this was a solid team with a skilled leader. I looked forward to learning from each one of them.

Trey strode over and held out a fist.

"Jay, we're glad you're joining us tonight."

Zion, Ruby, and Patricia all greeted me too.

I looked up at a towering tech whom I had never met before. The mountain of a man extended a huge, mahogany-hued hand. "I'm Jerome." His gravelly voice made him seem even bigger. I felt my anxiety evaporate. I knew I would be safe on his side. I tried not to stare at the scar under his right eye as Kavon came through the door and began hugging each one of us. Zion, Patricia, and I were so skinny he could have hugged us all at the same time. Ruby got a side hug because he couldn't stretch his arms out wide enough to give her a regular hug.

"I'm so happy y'all came," Kavon declared. "Now after report, while you work, I'm gonna watch the Steelers game."

Trey and Jerome rolled their eyes simultaneously.

"You don't even like the Steelers, Kavon," Trey pointed out.

"No, but you do," he replied. "And I like watching them lose."

As the last rays from the setting sun receded from the windows overlooking the crisis unit, Ruby sat at the male side desk. She stared at the clock, trying to wish it into the future by 15 minutes so she could finally take her break. A pale, gangly guy meandered over and asked her for some chapstick. Without a word or so much as a glance at him, she pulled open a drawer and handed him one. Don't worry, dear reader, it wasn't a crusty old used one. We stocked the drawers with basic hygiene supplies at the start of every shift specifically for the patients. In fact, we wished more of the patients would choose to actually use the hygiene products. The young man looked down at the chapstick she had slapped onto the desk in front of him.

"No, not that chapstick. The chapstick you're wearing."

She snatched the chapstick off the desk and threw it back in the drawer. "Go sit down now," she boomed. He looked down and trudged back to his seat.

Terry, a frequent flier, turned over in his recliner down the row and blared at him, "You just wanted one Peaceful Pines chapstick? I used to fill my bags with them and when I got out I sold them on the street."

I wondered who would buy chapstick that had come out of this place. When I pictured him pitching his hygiene products at the bus station, I tried not to think about what the nurses told me he did in the isolation room right in front of the security cameras.

I reflected on the juxtaposition of how I struggled to suppress my social anxiety enough to ask women for their phone numbers and here these guys in paper clothes had the shameless audacity to ask strangers crude questions. We're all crazy in some way or another.

Halfway through the shift, I wondered if anything worth writing about would happen by shift change. On my way back from escorting a patient out, I relished the beauty of the moonlight and the caress of the cool breeze. I stepped inside the unit and felt a surprising sense of serenity. The moon poured a deep blue across the dim common room. Aside from the occasional snore, the patients were as quiet as the rustling trees outside. The TV's on the walls were off. No bickering, or whining, or yelling at an ex over the phone. No slamming doors, no badgering for food, no chatter from the TV. I felt the knots in the back of my neck release as I wiped down the seat of the guy who got discharged. Crumbs filled every crevice. *Did he even get anything into his mouth*? I wondered. I was so aloof, that I hardly noticed Destiny, the charge nurse, standing outside the nurse station whispering to Trey.

Footsteps came behind me, and I spun around. Looking up into the eyes of a massive, baby-faced man. I stood at his shoulder level. His girth was twice mine. Fortunately, he wore green scrubs.

"'Scuse me, buddy, coming through." Allen squeezed through the aisle. "Who's the team lead?"

I nodded towards Trey and he headed over. I hardly realized how many techs were trickling in from other units or that they happened to be the biggest techs in the hospital. Deandre, Angel, and Jerome back from PER 2. *Odd. Maybe someone doesn't want to leave*, I thought. *Oh well, they would have told me if they needed me.* I went back to scrubbing away.

"RRRAAAAAA!" came an unintelligible burst of bellowing full of such panic and anger that it chilled my blood. Destiny opened the triage door, and Marva's strained voice came out.

"...aren't gonna do you no harm, but we need you to settle down before they take the handcuffs off."

As five towering techs filed into triage and out of view, a deep, frantic cry rang out.

"GET AWAY FROM ME! GET AWAY FROM ME!" it crescendoed into a howl.

Thump! "#%&@!" Bump! "GET AWAY!" Wump! "#%&@!" I had never heard anything like it from triage. It sounded like someone was throwing sacks of flour against the wall. Trey poked his head out and looked me in the eye. Sweat beaded across his forehead.

"Go get the taco!"

"From the cafeteria?" I stared back at him in confusion.

"Already got it." Destiny passed it to him. Apparently, the taco is a black padded tarp with handles used to carry patients like a tortilla carries carnitas. It's to keep staff out of patients' arms reach without dropping them. I stepped toward the door and Trey shook his head.

"There's no room in here. Go grab the restraints."

"Code Green PER!" rang out over the intercom.

"#%&@!" Another wump. Trey disappeared and the door clicked behind him.

"THEY'RE RAPING ME! THEY'RE RAPING ME!" resounded from inside.

The triage door swung unceremoniously open and Trey stumbled backwards into the room. He reached back in and emerged holding a handle of the taco. A huge leg from inside it kicked at him. Deandre strained on the other side gripping a handle. Jerome and Allen came through next each holding a side with both hands, sandwiching a thrashing woman inside. She looked about Allen's height, but twice his girth. The entire procession shook and jarred back and forth as she slapped and kicked at their hands.

"THEY'RE RAPING ME!" She thrashed again, landing a kick on Trey's hand. He lost his grip and the taco lurched, bringing Deandre to his knees. Allen and Jerome struggled to keep their end upright alee Trey's edge of the taco slapped against the floor and a huge lreg spilled out

.

"#%&@! Up on three!" Trey shouted. "One, two, *three*!" He and Deandre grunted and got back to their feet without getting kicked in the face.

Destiny knelt at the bed in the open quiet room, rapidly buckling the restraints in as I finished the other side. They nearly reached the quiet room door when–

"GET THE #%&@ AWAY FROM ME, #%&@S!"

The massive woman sat up in the taco. Shrieking, she grabbed Jerome's breast pocket. He braced and stood firm as she jerked her hand back, ripping the pocket clean off his scrub top. Pens flew in all directions and clattered around us. I heard the footsteps of the other techs running to the code coming behind them. Landon leaped into the scrum, pinning a leg while the other techs regained their grip.

"THEY'RE RAPING ME!"

Chantelle grabbed a handle next to Allen, whose face had turned red from exertion. I looked for a place to hold on, but there was no room. The mob of staff squeezed through the quiet room door, as they all lurched and stumbled in as if they were carrying a tornado.

"One, two, three!" Trey shouted. With a heave they hoisted the taco up and onto the bed and in unison they and all the reinforcements clamped down. Landon and Angel took a leg, Allen and Deandre took the other. Jerome held one arm down while I began to buckle the restraint onto her wrist. Chantelle and Destiny wrestled the other arm, but it wriggled out. Her free hand latched onto my collar and jerked down, bringing my face close to hers. My eyes widened. I had no idea what she would do now.

"I'LL KILL YOU!" She roared.

I tried standing up and pulling her hand off. I bobbed up momentarily but her firm grip had too much leverage for me. As her fist jerked me back down, her face loomed into mine. My mind froze. The woman opened her mouth. "TAKE THIS, #%&@!"

Suddenly, two hands latched onto her wrist, and wrenched her hand off my collar as some big hands pulled me back to my feet. There was no time to thank Jerome or Deandre. She still had a foot and a hand unbuckled. As Chantelle fumbled with the leg restraint, the free leg shook Landon back and forth. Deandre pinned the arm down and Jerome began buckling it when she began spitting in all directions. Everyone recoiled, and her hand swung back up. Deandre  pinned it back down, using his body weight as he turned his back to her.  The spittle splattered across the back of his scrubs. Ally came in with two syringes and dodged a stream of spittle. From the doorway, Patricia tossed me a towel. I knelt and held it up a foot above her face to shield us without smothering her. She still spat again and again at the other techs, but the towel caught each volley. A booming bellow reverberated through the tiny room as Ally jammed the needles into her hip. The woman's wild eyes met mine and she spat at me. I felt a fleck hit my eye as I turned my head. With that eye shut, I lowered the towel a few inches still well above her face and she continued to spit like a sprinkler. The last buckle clicked shut and the techs stood back, panting. The roars gradually turned into rumbles and she lay still as she fell into a sedated slumber.

Adrenaline still coursed through my veins. I trembled with nervous energy, ready to do something heroic, but I just needed to wash my face. As I dried my face, I realized that I couldn't imagine the trauma she must have gone through. She was really sick. I hoped they'd find the right treatment for her.

A week later on night shift, I was pushing the blood pressure monitor around the female side when the triage doors swung wide open.

"#%&@!" The police officers pushed a tall, lanky, handcuffed man through the triage doors. What looked like a nylon sock covered his head.

*Did they catch him in the middle of a robbery?* I wondered.

He pushed back at the officers with his shoulders. "I don't need your #%&@ING #%&@s! I'MA #%&@ YOU ALL UP!"

The officers shoved him into the nearest quiet room.

*What are they doing inside here?* I wondered.

As they unlocked the handcuffs, they sat him down and we techs pinned his arms and legs.

"We got it from here," Chantelle told them.

"We just need our spit guard and we'll get out of here," the officer replied. "Get ready to cover up."

"That's a spit guard? Where was that last week?" "Can we get one of those?" The questions poured out of my mouth.

"Nah, here we gotta keep the airway uncovered." Chantelle tossed me a towel.

*Here we go again,* I thought.

Chantelle snatched the stocking from his head as he spat fruitlessly in all directions. I was prepared this time, holding it low enough to protect my eyes without smothering him.

The officers went back to triage to retrieve their guns from the lockbox. As Ally strolled in with a syringe in each hand, I wondered if they locked up their guns to keep them out of patients' hands from theory or experience.

Ally worked her magic and placed a band-aid over the injection site.

I turned to her. "I'm gonna start calling you the sand woman, you put everyone to sleep."

"Yep, you better watch your back," came the reply.

❊ ❊ ❊

Ruby sat at the desk on the female side, feverishly checking in new patients when a wide-eyed, middle-aged man moseyed over. "Hey, hey, hey, can you show me how to use Facebook?"

She raised an eyebrow and looked around, wondering how he was going to access Facebook if his phone had been confiscated. The long line of new arrivals had already worn her patience thin, and she didn't have much to begin with.

"What you want to use Facebook for?" She queried in consternation, picking up a locked crate and slamming it onto the desk.

"So I can look you up when I get home," he replied. Her eyebrow rose up even farther.

"What makes you think I have a Facebook?" She retorted as she ripped the unfortunate zip ties off the box with her bare hands.

The man looked down at the unrecognizable remains of the zip tie and gulped. This had gone much better when he imagined it five minutes ago. He had to impress her fast before he got kicked back to the other side.

"When I get a job, you can have my whole paycheck," he blurted out. His lips flickered into a grin. *That was a good one, I'll have to use it more often,* he told himself.

"Then you can come back when you got a job." Her

glowering glare evaporated his grin. He slunk away, praying that no one he knew was there to overhear her.

# CHAPTER 12: **CHEWED OUT**

When I walked into the break room at the start of the next night shift, Betsy, the charge nurse, told me, "The shift Supervisor assigned you to 2."

"Unit 2, isn't that the women's unit?"

"Yeah, but they're short-staffed. We'll miss you. Please come back."

"Of course, I love it over here." *Hopefully, my partner has already been there.* If neither of us were familiar with the patients, then they could catch us with all sorts of surprises. You don't get much time to learn their quirks, what works with them, and what sets them off without actually setting them off. I grabbed my backpack and hustled over. I didn't want to miss report on a bunch of patients I had never met before. I walked in and saw Brenda at the tech desk as Landon paced the unit in the vest. *That's a relief* I thought. Brenda was down to earth and a hard worker.

"Hey, Brenda! I didn't know you switched to night shift. Do you want me to take the vest first or get vital signs?"

"Oh, hi Jay. Actually, I'm on day shift. It's you and Landon tonight."

I looked at Landon, a scrawny white guy like myself. Fortunately, he had a buzz cut so nobody would confuse us with each other.

"You're tellin' me they put two males to cover the female? What were they thinking?"

"I know, Landon—I mean Jay. You two look just like each other."

Landon and I looked at each other, wondering which one of us should be offended by that comment.

"At least both the nurses are female."

Landon piped up, "Stacey, the unit manager, said that the female patients always keep calm with the male staff and the male patients always keep calm with the female staff but not vice versa." As the patients slept, whoever wore the vest on the unit had to check on them and prove they did so by tagging a flashlight-sized tube against the metal receiver bolted to the wall in every room. I was horrified they would send a female to go inside the rooms to check on the men and vice versa.

"But what if the women have PTSD? Having a guy go in their room every hour would just trigger them," I questioned.

"Sometimes the nurses will help if they're the other gender."

"But only if you're nice to them and bring them soda." Patty the nurse boomed from across the room, before chuckling to herself.

Landon placed a hand on my shoulder. "Look, it doesn't matter what gender you are. One time I was doing rounds in 4 and I went to tag the receiver on the wall and this guy comes out of nowhere and punches me in the back of the head. He'd been waiting for me behind the door."

"So how'd you get out?" I asked from the edge of my seat.

Unimpressed, Brenda smirked, "That explains why you are the way you are."

Landon's brow furrowed. "Ain't it time for you to go already? We got work to do."

Brenda turned to leave. "Good luck, Jay. I hope you get punched again, Landon."

As she left, I turned a quizzical glance to Landon. "What happened between you two?"

"She's best friends with my ex."

"And?"

"I don't want to talk about it."

"It's going to be a long shift, Landon."

"You were asking what happened after I got punched in the back of the head. I landed on the ground and jumped up and he was between me an' the door. I held that wand-pipe thing like a bat and he stood his distance. You know that nurse from 4 that's built like a pro wrestler?"

"Davis? Yeah."

"He heard the commotion and came in the door behind the guy and bear-hugged him and we pinned him down. Luckily that patient didn't have a roommate or it woulda been two on one for a minute."

Patty piped up, "You forgot to mention the part where you scream—" Patty switched to a falsetto–'Help! Help! Help!' as you pounded the wall with your little fist."

"Who told you that? I mean, that's a big exaggeration." Landon paused awkwardly then grabbed the binder and flipped it open.

"You missed report, look here, that's Becky,  she's hard of hearing so she's loud but not aggressive. Everyone is used to it by now. We just need to remember that Eva's allergic to peanuts at snack time. That's it."

"Easy peezy."

"Don't jinx us on our first night together, Jay."

I couldn't tell if he was kidding or not. Chuckling, I asked, "You want me to start with the vest or the vital signs?"

We got settled in when a young, well-groomed woman with short black hair walked up. She had an Asian appearing complexion.

"Can you please open the bathroom for me?"

"Sure," I replied.

We started walking toward the locked door.

"I'm Jay, what's your name?"

"Katie. You should know there's two Katie's here. I'm Katie Fields."

"Thanks for the heads up." I turned the key and opened the door for her.

"Thank you, Jay."

Around 9:00 PM, Landon went into the kitchen to prepare

the nighttime snacks while I monitored the unit. The patients lined up in front of the door as soon as they saw him go inside.

He pushed out a catering cart with bins of string cheese, milk, crackers, and red delicious apples. I love passing out snacks when there's enough for everybody. There's something satisfying about seeing people get some nourishment. Plus, it makes everybody happy. Just about everybody. One woman in a white poncho eagerly reached for an apple.

"Hold up, let me lock the kitchen," Landon said authoritatively.

She flushed and stepped back. It must be her first night here. He turned the key with a 'Click.'

"Alright, ladies first, one at a time, everyone picks two things so everybody gets a choice, then you can come back for more."

They obliged, and I held back my surprise at how smoothly this was going until—

"Hey, that's three things," Landon interjected. "Put one back."

A slender woman, hair wrapped in a bandana, stared Landon down. She clutched three cheese sticks.

"I'm real hungry."

"You see all them?" He pointed at the line behind her. "They're hungry, too. You've been here enough times to know better. Put one back and wait your turn."

She rolled her eyes and tossed the extra cheese stick at him. It bounced off his chest and onto the floor. He didn't even look at it.

"Okay then, no seconds for you. Next!"

Halfway through the line, Katie Fields dug through the bowl of apples.

"You don't need to touch all of them," Landon pointed out.

Her head snapped up from the bowl.

"I want a green apple, please."

"We have ripe red delicious apples here."

"But I want a green apple, PLEASE."

"You'll have to wait for everyone else in line and then I can go check and see if we have green apples in the fridge."

She crossed her arms. I could almost see the steam emitting from her ears.

*Time to put out the embers before we get a forest fire.* I tossed Landon the vest. "Here, I'll go back and check so you can finish here."

He casually slung it over his shoulder.

I unlocked the kitchen, jumped inside, and—*click*—*locked it behind me before swinging open the fridge door.*

*Rows of milk, drawer of cheese, some yogurt, deli sandwiches, bananas, oranges.*" I scanned again but still no green apples. I stuck my head back out.

"Hey Katie, I'm sorry, but we don't have any green apples in the fridge. I can see about something else, how about a banana or an orange?"

She glared. "Those aren't a green apple. I said I want a *green* apple."

Landon and I exchanged glances. This was getting ridiculous.

"Alright, I can check the cabinets to see if one got stuck there but I can't promise you anything."

She nodded and began to tap her foot. Watching her hover over the cart, the next people in line just stood there, wide-eyed, afraid to approach the cart no matter how hungry they felt. I leaped inside the kitchen and threw open the cabinets. Cups, disposable forks, straws, paper towels, Superman action figure—*wait how'd that get here? Oh well, I'll have to find out later.* I dumped out the entire contents of the cabinets onto the counter. No green apple. My heart dropped to my stomach. I had an inkling of what would happen next. I came back out and fumbled with the keys, desperately stalling for time. Surrendering to fate, I turned and held up my open hands.

"Katie I'm sorry but I looked all over and we just don't have any. If we did, I'd give it to you for sure."

143

"*What?*" She replied, "DO YOU EVEN KNOW WHAT GREEN IS? I SAID I WANT A GREEN APPLE. GIVE ME A # %&@ING GREEN APPLE NOW!"

"CODE GREEN Unit 2" Patty's voice echoed over the intercom.

"RRRRRAAAAAA!!! I SAID A GREEN APPLE, NOT A GREEN *CODE*!"

The next people in line simultaneously took another step back.

Landon and I positioned ourselves between her and the other patients.

"EVERYONE TO YOUR ROOMS! IT'LL BE A MINUTE," Landon shouted.

The other patients silently shuffled to their rooms, but no one shut the door. They all stood peering out at the unfolding drama.

At this point, we had nothing to lose, so I took a shot. "Hey, Katie, I see you're really frustrated right now. You really want that green apple. Why don't we sit down over there and talk about it?"

"I'm not frustrated. I'M PISSED. GIVE ME A #%&@ING GREEN APPLE RIGHT NOW!"

"Look, if you can't calm down, we can't go look for a green apple," Landon chimed in.

"I'M SICK OF THIS #%&@! IF I DON'T GET A GREEN APPLE I'M GONNA #%&@ THIS PLACE UP!" She grabbed the cart. Landon anticipated her intent and lunged for it. She yanked down and it tottered on two wheels but stayed there, suspended. Pulling from the opposite direction, Landon held it back from toppling over. She shot a furious glare at him.

"YOU #%&@ING WHITE BOY. GO GET A GREEN APPLE!" She then shoved the cart towards Landon who was still pulling back. He stumbled back and the cart crashed onto its side, spilling its contents across the room. Cartons of milk burst around our feet, cheese sticks skidded in all directions across the floor and wrong-colored apples rolled about. Forget what I said about having nothing to lose.

"THAT'S WHAT YOU GET!" Katie shouted, her fists clenched.

Ruby and Chantelle led a wave of green scrubs through the unit door and surrounded the three of us.

"Are you the one that wanted a green apple?" Chantelle asked Katie.

"Yes."

"Well, we got a nice green apple for ya in that room over there." Without another word, Ruby and Chantelle each took one of Katie's arms and escorted her toward the room.

"I can walk by myself," Katie growled.

"We're almost there,  honey." Ruby replied. They pushed her into the room, followed by several more techs, and lastly, Patty who held two capped syringes. Katie howled and swore at everyone in the room, their mothers,  and their dogs; then went quiet. The staff slowly filed out. Ruby turned to Chantelle.

"Do you think she'll dream of getting a green apple?"

After sorting out snacks and convincing everyone to go to their rooms, we sat quietly in the empty unit floor.

I got up and walked around, trying to keep my droopy eyes alert, when "CODE GREEN UNIT 4" blared over the intercom. My eyes snapped wide open.

"Hey Landon, do you mind if I take this one?"

"Go for it, but I got the next one."

Delighted, I ran out the door through the annex. As I rushed into the breezeway to four and swung open the unit door to find dimly lit spooky silence.  Where was the yelling? The wrestling? The death threats? Just a row of paper neatly lined up on the floor, each with different markings and different colors.  I saw Patricia and Allen standing a few paces away from a slender, well-dressed young woman with dark eyes, disheveled short black hair and copper-toned skin. She didn't turn or even notice as I came in followed by Allen and Chantelle. She just kept a thousand-yard stare as if she was shell-shocked.

"This is Joy. She's not dangerous, just wakin' everybody up," Allen whispered. "She won't have anything to do with Patricia or me." Her gaze swept across the crowd of us techs trickling in. Chantelle stepped forward, gently reaching out her hand.

"Hi honey, are you feelin' okay?" she asked Joy.

"Get back, demon!" Joy swatted Chantelle's hand away. Her gaze remained aloof as if she were blind. "Demons, demons, all of you are demons," she declared as she pointed at the crowd of techs. "I need an angel. Where's an angel? All of you are demons. Except you, you're an angel."

She slowly grabbed onto my sleeve and softly pulled. I stepped beside her, feeling flattered.

"Here, hold this." She handed me one of the papers with mysterious markings.

"Hey Joy, can you tell me about your pictures here?" I asked.

She still stared off into the distance. "I need another angel."

A couple more techs walked in from the other side and stopped as surprise filled their faces. They weren't expecting this any more than I was.

"An angel, I need another angel."
Chantelle grabbed the shoulder of one of the techs that had just walked in and pushed him forward.

"Here's another angel."

"You're an angel?" Hope asked him.

"Yeah, it says it here on my badge." His name was Angel.

"Okay, hold this." She handed him a paper.

My jaw hit the floor. *What are the chances?* I wondered. *It's like a movie or something. No one would believe me if I wrote about it.*

Joy handed him another paper.

Patty, the nurse came from behind us holding a capped syringe in each hand. "I've got her meds ready, can you get her to the quiet room?" Since the shot goes in the muscle right under the hip, we always tried to give the shots in privacy.

"Hey, Hope, let's take these pictures over there, we can tape them to the wall," Angel suggested.

Her blank stare turned toward the quiet room. "Over there?"

"Yes, over there." Angel and I each placed a hand on her shoulder and gently guided her toward the room. She walked slowly, as if she was in slow motion. She was really sick.

"Okay Hope, Patty has some medicine to help you feel better," Angel continued.

"Medicine?"

Angel and I each held an elbow and a shoulder to keep her from hitting Patty, who deftly lowered the edge of Hope's pants, wiped off the corner of her hip, and jammed both needles in at the same time. Hope flinched, gasped, but didn't flail. She did better than most of the gang-bangers I'd seen get shots in PER. We guided Hope to sit down on the bed.

"Alright guys, I can get it from here," Patricia told us. She looked relieved.

"Alright Hope, we're going to give you some space, see you later," I told her.

A few days later, during day shift, I waited in the lunch line at the cafeteria, trying to convince my hunger to hang on. Brenda brought in the patients from 4 that were cleared to go eat at the cafeteria.

*I got here just in time*, I thought. *A couple minutes later and I would be waiting behind twelve people.*

"Hello there, how's your day going?" A female voice came from behind me.

I turned and did a double take. It was Joy, but a completely new Joy. She looked me in the eye, friendly, smiling. Her hair was done up and she had even put on makeup, doing a better job than some of my coworkers.

"It's good, ready for lunch. How are you today?"

She beamed "Much better. It's so nice to come out of the

unit and the food is better here too."

"Hey baby, do you want ribs or pork chops?" the cook, Violet, asked from behind the glass protecting our lunch from any sneezes. Ideally. The glass was a strip at chest height. A sneeze from a short person could cover everything.

"Oh, some ribs for sure." Violet plopped some ribs on her plate.

"What sides and dessert?"

"For sides, I want coleslaw and mixed veggies. For dessert, oh-umm, they all look good. How about the chocolate cake?"

The Joy I had met earlier wasn't capable of a lucid conversation. Witnessing such a dramatic change shocked me. It was definitely rewarding to see that some patients actually got better on the units. I overthought what to say, wondering if she even recognized me or had any clue about her psychotic episode.

Joy picked up her tray. "Well, I'm going to go eat with some of my new friends. Have a good one."

"You too."

Now she was one of those bubbly people you run into every day at the store, the library, school, etc. The "normal" people I interacted with outside of Peaceful Pines surely harbored their own secret challenges. Just because someone gets sick doesn't mean they're incapable of getting better. I thought back to my previous job, where I dreaded going to work each day. The manager there treated me graciously at the interview but I later saw what lay behind his masquerade. Just because someone looks well and normal on the surface doesn't mean they're incapable of doing sick things.

* * *

I left for a week to see my fiancée—that's another story —and returned back in time for another night shift. So, it went smoothly—which means boring. I ran back and forth along the back row, cleaning up the bathrooms and restocking. I kept hearing mumbling as I went back and forth. It was Jill, a petite, blonde girl in the back row. She sat sideways on her recliner, legs hanging over the armrest, talking to herself.

"Do you need anything, Jill?" I asked. Without even looking at me she stopped mumbling just long enough to say "No thanks" before going back to talking to herself.

*At least she's quiet*, I thought to myself. If I had said that out loud, my coworkers would have berated me for cursing our shift with the q-word. *Silly superstitions.*

Halfway through mid-shift we still had nothing more exciting than busy work as I took my turn as monitor. Nothing more than writing where every patient was.

Destiny came out of the nurse station and handed me a patient's chart.

"Jill's going to Unit 2," she told me.

"Oh good, she's been quiet. Now she'll get to relax in the good behavior unit," I replied.

"Careful with the q-word," Destiny replied.

"Quiet, quiet, quiet," I replied as I jotted down another routine round.

An hour later, I heard shouts by the nurse's window.

"NO WAY I'M GOING, YOU HEAR ME! I DON'T WANT TO DIE!!"

Not surprised, I looked up to see who it was. Then I was surprised. *Jill? What happened to that mild-mannered girl?* I wondered.

Jill bellowed, with clenched fists raised at an open nurse station window. Ally, the nurse behind the window, attempted to console her, only to get another round of shouting in her face.

"WHAT? ARE YOU TRYING TO KILL ME?" Suddenly Jill swung a fist through the open window at Ally's head. Fortunately, Ally reflexively dodged it and backed out of the way before closing the window. As soon as I saw Jill swing, I cautiously walked their way, not waiting to trigger an explosion by rushing toward her.

Dee, one of the kindest nurses on PER, stepped out of the station and headed towards the female side desk. As soon as Jill saw her come onto the floor, she dashed over to Dee and blindsided her with a haymaker.

*Not Dee! That's it!* I told myself. I dashed over. As Jill turned to face me, I over-under-hooked her arms in a classic wrestling hold. I was comfortable like that because I knew she couldn't hit anybody now. Comfortable that is until she chomped down on my cheek. I pulled my face away but she only bit down harder. I'd never been in this dilemma before. Biting is against the rules in wrestling, MMA, and boxing. PER had no referee to disqualify her here. It was up to me to adapt. I waited for her to let go so I could pull away. She didn't. My mind raced, *"If I push or pull myself away, it will rip my cheek."* Then I recalled my mother teaching me to squeeze my baby brother's jaw muscles in order to sweep things out of his mouth. I gave it a try, but she had clamped down like a bulldog.

*What else can I do?* I racked my brain. As my teammates surrounded us, anxious to help, I felt her tense up more and she bit down with all her might. Usually, a swarm of staff members can pin violent patients down without thinking twice but how could they separate us without separating my face? They exchanged befuddled glances. Nobody had trained us for this. Nobody knew what to do. *I wouldn't be here if I had just stayed on vacation one more day*, I told myself.

Eventually, after my adrenaline simmered, I realized she must be scared of what would happen if she let go. In order to draw her out of fight-or-flight mode, I began talking to her in a calm voice. "It's okay, Jill, you're not in trouble. You're going to be fine."

After what felt like minutes of me talking while the other staff still exchanged worried glances, wondering what to do, Jill let go. Immediately they grabbed her arms from either side and escorted her to the quiet room. I looked up at Ally.

"Nice reflexes back there, Ally. Can you take the vest so I

can wash my face?"

"Yeah, no problem. She got you pretty good. Use plenty of soap."

I rushed inside and saw no blood in the sink as I cleaned my cheek. I went back out and into the nurse's station.

"Let me see your face," Jackie told me inside the nurse station. As I turned her jaw dropped. "#%&@!"

"You're not very comforting," I replied.

"Yeah, that's bad," chirped Destiny.

"They're going to send you next door [to the medical hospital]," Jackie told me.

"Really?"

I ran back into the break room to take a picture and see for myself.

"Not as bad as I thought," I mused observing the key-sized streak of dark red blood oozing just below my cheekbone.

"*Well this is cool, great story, perfect for a book,*" I told myself. "*I almost missed this. I got back from vacation just in time.*"

I returned and Destiny bandaged the bite wound.

"Andre said he's putting together the paperwork for you to go to the Emergency Room next door."

"For this little thing?"

Dr. Miller swiveled in his seat, which let out a groan. "Yes, you're going to need a round of antibiotics."

Noting my puzzled face he elaborated, "Out of all the mammals, bear and human mouths are the filthiest. Bears have anaerobic bacteria."

Destiny looked over at me and grinned. "I don't think you'll care about what bacteria it is after a bear bite. Do you want us to call an ambulance and they can drive you?"

"You can't be serious," I replied.

After returning from the ER next door, I reported to the shift supervisor's office. As I opened the door, the silver-haired assistant supervisor, Nathan, looked up with a sympathetic half-smile.

"What'd they do for you?"

"Just a couple prescriptions. The PA said it didn't need stitches," I replied in disappointment. If someone was going to bite my face, they might as well make it look impressive.

"I'm sorry that happened to you. Why don't you take a seat?" He came from behind his desk and plopped down on a sunken sofa seat next to me. "Back in the day I was on a code where a patient bit the back of a nurse's ankle and wouldn't let go. She was screaming. When we were getting him in restraints he got me right here," he said, pointing to his inner thigh.

"I got home and it was a bruise with a chunk torn out, I'm just glad it wasn't any higher." He paused, possibly for laughter.

I didn't want to risk laughing at my supervisor's near castration.

When the shift supervisor, Helen, arrived, I recounted what just happened in PER. She looked at the ceiling and sighed. "At least she didn't climb through the [nurse station] window. We had a guy do that a few months ago."

*Where's the sympathy?* I wondered silently.

"You better go pick up those antibiotics right now. CVS over on Central Avenue is open 24 hours," she continued.

During the next shift, people kept asking me if I was okay, concern emitting from their eyes as if the patient had chewed my arm off and given me hepatitis. Whenever I get scratches and scabs I usually make up some crazy story about wrestling saber-toothed tigers. I planned to do that when people asked about my face, but then I realized that the truth was crazy enough.

"What happened to your face?" Landon asked the next day.

"I was born this way, you jerk. Not everyone can be beautiful," I replied.

After dropping off a patient at unit 2, Chantelle and Patty asked me what happened last night. I told them.

"To you? You're the nicest guy." Chantelle told me. "If I was there I woulda-bam-shown her what's what."

When I dropped off another patient at Unit 1, I recognized a patient from PER the night before. He was a middle-aged, well-fed man with glasses and a cream colored complexion.

"Hi Mike," I greeted him.

"Hi, Jay. How's your face?"

"Mike told me what happened last night," a spindly young guy cut in. "He had a front-row seat. It was Jill that bit you, wasn't it?"

"What?" I didn't realize the patients exchanged gossip so quickly.

"Mike told me he saw it," his pasty face broke into a grin as he pointed to the well-fed fellow across from him.

"You alright?" the well-fed fellow asked. "You kept calm the whole time. I woulda freaked out. I'm impressed."

"Did Jill bite you? Was it her?" interjected the skinny young man.

"I'm not naming any names," I replied with a grin.

"Well, I know it was her because she was my girlfriend and she bit me."

It's a small world in psychiatry.

As I drove home, I recalled what the recruiter, Lori, had told me when I asked about this position. "It's not for everybody... ...they don't last long."

I didn't think to ask her why they didn't last long. For that matter, I didn't last long at my old job. Lori took a chance on me. Some might even call her crazy for letting me try.

The patients at my old job were quiet, calm, and collected. I loved serving them. The doctors were the only ones that yelled there. One even chewed out—figuratively—the unit supervisor in the hallway so loudly that the patients he was about to operate on got spooked.

"I-is he okay?" they asked, wondering if the doctor needed a ride to PER.

The next morning I called the angel recruiter up. "Hi Lori, this is Jay, you probably don't remember me, but I just wanted to say thanks for getting me this job. You took a chance on me and it's a great fit. I love it. I can't thank you enough."

"Oh," she replied in shock. "I appreciate that very much... ...is there anything you need?"

"Um... no, I just wanted to say thanks," I answered, realizing that most people only told her thank you when they wanted something from her.

"Wow, well let me know if there ever is anything I can do for you."

"Will do."

I still can't thank her enough. I've always wanted to work at a psychiatric hospital. If I hadn't asked her about it, then 'What if?' would still be gnawing at my mind to this day. It would have been so easy to tell myself, like so many times before, that "She'll probably say no. There's no way this would work out." Instead, I asked myself, "What if it did work out?" and "What's the worst that could happen?" Fortunately for me, I realized that I probably wouldn't lose life or limb if she said no.

"What if?" is a tool we can use to either launch ourselves to a new world or imprison ourselves in a cage of anxiety and doubt. What's something that you've always wanted to do, dear reader? Please skip this part if you are some kind of sociopath who obsesses about hurting people. Now, for those of you who are left, if any, what if you tried doing what you have always dreamed of doing and it worked out? What's the worst that could happen? Is it worse than leaving yourself wondering what might have happened? Are you sick of my questions yet? I promise to stop asking questions if you stop procrastinating and take that first step toward whatever it is that you've always wanted to do but haven't.*

*Reader discretion is advised. You agree to do so at your own risk and take full responsibility for the outcome. If you have no common sense, ask a responsible, trusted adult who does have common sense if this is right for you. By reading this paragraph, you are agreeing not to hold me liable for any adverse outcomes including but not limited to injury, financial or emotional loss, death, amputation, spontaneous combustion, or the apocalypse that may result.*

Let's end on a positive note. Be it the clerk at the grocery store, the waiter at the restaurant, someone supporting the wrong politician, or even that idiot who cut me off in traffic this morning and deserves to have their license revoked, car crushed, and their nose hairs plucked out one by one—sorry, I got a little carried away there. Let me try that again.

We have no idea what challenges the people around us are going through. Sometimes the ones closest to us, no matter what their social media may portray, suffer silently behind a facade they fear tearing down. Sometimes you know something is up with a loved one, but you don't know what to say.

An attorney sat stuck in traffic on the way to his demanding job, when he got a call from his friend's wife. Her husband was in crisis. She asked if he could go be with him while they waited for additional help to arrive. My friend took the next exit, told his boss he had an emergency, and went straight there. Sitting there with his friend, he scrambled to come up with the right thing to say. It felt awkward and overwhelming. To make it worse, his phone kept buzzing and he had to keep silencing it.

Later, his friend told him, "Thanks for coming, it made a big difference."

Remembering how inadequate he felt, my friend replied, "What did I say that actually helped?"

His friend replied, "I don't remember anything that you said. I just remember that your phone kept buzzing and you would silence it and put it back in your pocket. You were there for me."

You may not be a psychologist that knows everything, but you don't have to be one to make a difference. As someone who has been there, trust me, something as simple as a smile, a pause to ask how they're doing, or telling a dad joke can go a long way. You don't have to have a degree to do any of those things. What does it take for someone to be worthy of any of those things? Does it take anything at all? Do they have to share one's religion or political party? Dehumanizing others who are different may provide a false sense of security, but in reality it is poison. Despite his suffering in a concentration camp, Viktor Frankl pointed out:

"Each of us carries a unique spark of the divine, and each of us is also an inseparable part of the web of life."

An investment in the social and mental health of others is an investment in one's own wellbeing. It does not mean one completely agrees with or approves of or even trusts the recipient.

Our circumstances, our health, or lack thereof, do not define us. Viktor Frankl survived the Holocaust, but not every holocaust survivor is Viktor Frankl—because he is more than a holocaust survivor. Just because someone feels depressed doesn't mean they *are* depression. If someone is a certain age, or on the autism spectrum, or in a wheelchair; they are still first and foremost Someone. Just because someone participates in a certain political party or religion does not mean they *are* that religion or political party. They are something more, still a person. They too have regrets, fears, and hopes. They too get hungry and cold just like you do. Most want love and peace like you do. Most of all, each person is human just like you, a member of the human family.

# ACKNOWLEDGEMENTS

This book would not exist without:

Gaby Smith, my better half
Heather Smith, underpaid chief editor who allowed me to live
Jenny Hess, underpaid editor
Colette Aburime, founder of WritingWithColor
Anonymous recruiter, who allowed to me try

Printed in Great Britain
by Amazon

37464664R00096